PUSHING
UP DAISIES

Coco Kristine

Printed in the United States of America

First Printing: Aug 2017
Wenner Publishing Company

ISBN 9781549625176

I dedicate this book to Sarah "Sally" Skahen, the one who kept hope alive in my heart even in the darkest of times.

CHAPTER ONE:

Dad sighed as we pulled through the third wrought-iron gate of the ancient cemetery on the west side of town. He drove up the icy path and turned onto the still frozen grass. He passed the small chapel and solitary mausoleums, to the plot with the piled, upturned dirt of the newly dug grave.

My stomach twisted in agony at the sight.

I couldn't handle this.

The hum of the engine died, and Dad pulled his hat over what remained of his thin, black hair. "I'm sorry about your friend, Mimi. I wish things could have turned out differently." He switched off the *Wig Wag* system as he spoke.

"She wrapped her car around a telephone pole, Dad, there's no other outcome," I replied bitterly, wrapping my black pea-coat around me tighter. Looking out the slightly frosted window, I pushed my long, black hair out of my swollen, gold eyes and waited for him to reply.

He sighed again before silently opening the door and stepping out into the cold, unforgiving rain of late March.

I bit my trembling lip and looked out the window at the pitiful scene, my breath fogging up the glass.

"Mimi, it's all going to be alright, I'll be next to you the entire time." Jenny was sitting next to me now, her long blond curls hanging in her face the way vines do on the side of buildings.

"And what good will that do me? No one can even see you but me; to everyone else, you're dead." The next round of tears began to flow as I suppressed the sob that was rising in my sore throat.

Jenny turned and looked out the window. "I don't feel dead though, I mean, you can see me and hear me, it's not like that much has changed."

"Other than the fact that my family thinks I'm grief-stricken and crazy because I keep talking about you as if you were still alive because you refuse to crossover," I mumbled icily.

"Well, look at the bright side; I've always wanted to go to my own funeral. Even in death I'm insanely popular!" She grinned broadly at me then began a fruitless attempt to push me into the window. "Now hurry up! I don't want to miss my burial!"

"Right, because everyone wants to see their body lowered into the ground," I answered sarcastically, grabbing the door handle.

"Exactly!" she agreed. "But seriously, what good is seeing and talking to ghosts if there are no ghosts to be found?"

"You're a horrible person," I told her angrily, letting go of the handle.

"Ghost, actually, I'm dead. Remember?" Jenny gladly pointed out. She stuck her hand through my stomach for emphasis.

There was a knock on my window, and I looked out to see a tall figure with short, messy, auburn hair and thick, black-rimmed glasses, hopping up and down like a jackrabbit outside. I quickly opened the door, feeling the icy blast of frozen air shoot through into the interior of the old hearse, and scooted over as Charlie clambered into the seat next to me.

"Good God! Jenny sure chose a horrible day for a funeral," he remarked as he took off his glasses and rubbed off the fog.

"I thought it was fitting," Jenny replied with a smile.

"Hell, she'd probably think it was fitting, raining and cold, the ground not wanting to gobble her up. It would be just her style," Charlie continued as he slid his glasses back onto his nose, not taking any notice to Jenny's remark.

"You have no idea," I replied ironically.

Charlie shrugged and smiled at me. I could see that his eyes were still red and that this was most likely the first time he'd smiled all day. "Do you think she's still with us?" he asked me in a more serious, almost pleading, tone.

"Of course I'm here! I'm sitting right next to you, Charlie!" Jenny reached out her hand and turned on the radio. Suddenly, the car filled with Queen's irritating tumult:

Another one bites the dust,
Another one bites the dust,
And another one gone,
And another one gone,
Another one bites the dust–

Charlie cried out in alarm as I quickly turned off the radio that surged with her unnatural energy.

"Sorry, it's an old hearse," I lied quickly, throwing an accusing glance at Jenny, who merely shrugged.

Charlie stared at the radio and shook his freckly head. "Ha ha, right, old hearse." He laughed uncertainly. Despite the fact that Charlie and I were good friends, I kept from him my ability to see the dead, figuring that he'd find me crazy if he ever found out. I mean, it's not like he'd be the first.

"We should go or else they may begin the prayer without us," I said, quickly changing the subject before Charlie could mull over it any further.

He nodded his head wearily then opened the door, allowing the last of the warm air to be sucked from the vehicle. "I hate how everything is supposed to go back to normal tomorrow when we get to school," he said bitterly as he stepped out of the low door.

"I know, it doesn't seem right," I agreed, following him out into the rain.

"And the worst part; a new kid is coming in! It's as if they're trying to replace her and it isn't fair!" Charlie spat on the ground.

I put my arm around his tall figure and silently led him to the large group of mourners. "I know, but life isn't fair."

"I still don't agree with it." He stared at his feet in silence as we slowly walked towards the rest of the mourners.

CHAPTER TWO:

Beep. Beep. Beep.

My alarm went off and I hit the snooze button, rolling over onto my side. Was it six-thirty already? I readjusted the blankets and closed my eyes, hoping to catch a few more z's before I had to begin preparing for school in a few hours.

The attempt was futile. Jenny had been waiting anxiously for the alarm to go off. "Hold it right there, Mimi!" Her voice sounded like a buzzer. "You've got school!"

"Since when are you my mother?" I groaned, pulling the thick blue covers over my head.

"GET UP!" Jenny yelled and the light in my room exploded.

I threw the covers off and slid out into the cold air of the room. "Why'd you have to destroy the light bulb?" I asked, not hiding the annoyance in my voice.

"Maybe if you'd gotten up, it wouldn't have gone *bang!* It's all your fault." Jenny crossed her slim arms across her chest. She remained ageless; forever the image of her former sixteen-year-old self. Her blonde hair curled down her back, her red lips curved into an accusing smile that she had perfected over the years, and her clothes were the same as they had been the day she died; black leather hooker boots, dark-blue skinny jeans, and her favorite silky red blouse.

Looking at her always sent a wave of guilt over me like it was my fault she died. She was my ghost, the one haunting me. We all have ghosts—a past memory of something we regret, an event we could have prevented—Jenny was mine. Seeing her every day was my punishment.

"You're staring at me, again," Jenny blurted out, bringing my thoughts back to reality.

"Can't a person stare at a ghost?" I asked slyly as I slipped on the blue bunny slippers that I'd received for my twelfth birthday. I began to pick my way to the door, over all the books and clothes that I had neglected to pick up, hoping to not step on fragments of the shattered light.

"No, it's not natural!" Jenny called after me.

"If you haven't noticed, I'm pretty unnatural," I replied, not turning my head as I opened the door and peered out into the hallway. I sighed with relief; nobody was up.

"Right, you're ghost girl," Jenny joked, gliding over into the hallway.

I raised my eyebrows. "I'm not the one who can walk through walls."

"Shut up."

Laughing, I flipped on the light switch in the hallway and began getting ready for school.

I threw on a shirt and pair of jeans at random, not caring whether they matched or not. Mom would yell at me if I needed to change hopefully.

Getting ready for school was a bit of a blur; one second, I was brushing my hair, the next, I had completed my eyeliner and mascara. A part of me thought that I probably shouldn't have done the eye makeup, but it was too late now.

I slowly shuffled downstairs to the kitchen to pour myself a bowl of cereal. Mom and Dad were standing around the coffee pot, so they didn't hear my entrance. I walked over to the fridge and opened it, searching for the milk. There was none of course.

"We're out of milk," I said with a sigh. Today was not going to be a great day, I could feel it.

"Mimi, I didn't see you come in," Mom told me, her hand on her heart as if I'd frightened her.

"Sorry," I mumbled, not really in the mood to talk.

"I didn't expect to see you this morning," Dad chimed in. He was dressed in his work suit, probably getting ready to meet a family or something.

"I have school," I replied, putting the cereal back in the cupboard.

"Are you certain you want to go? You could stay home a few more days," Mom insisted, walking over with a cup of coffee poured for me.

I accepted the coffee with a silent nod. "I don't want to fall further behind," I told her. "I'm fine, seriously."

They exchanged a look, and I knew they didn't believe me. I didn't believe me. But they let it go and we all drank our coffee in silence.

* * *

So, the first day back at school after the funeral was . . . awkward. No one would look me in the eye, and if we accidentally made eye-contact, they would shift theirs away guiltily, mumbling their condolences to the tiled floor of the school building. It would have been fine, but I wasn't the only one receiving this treatment, and Charlie couldn't handle it.

"It's as if we died in that car accident with Jenny!" he told me during lunch, and he was right, it was like we were dead.

For some reason, nobody knew how to say, "I'm sorry your friend died, she was a good person." Seriously, how hard is it to say that?! But Jenny was the first kid to have died in our school ever; she was the first in over one-hundred years. Even the teachers didn't know how to broach the subject. Dying is for the old, not for kids.

Jenny wasn't much of a help either. She stalked me the entire day, never leaving my side and continuously babbling about how she expected everyone to be crying over her death. "Why aren't they giving you two hugs and telling you about how great a person Jennifer Goodridge was? I feel so insulted!"

I did my best to ignore her, but by Chemistry class, it was near impossible. Jenny had been my lab partner before she died, and she was determined to continue being so even in death. She sat in her chair at our lab table, putting her feet up on the table and humming "Baby Got Back" by Sir Mix-A-Lot. I sat in my chair, trying to take notes on what the lab was for the day, when the teacher was interrupted by a knock at the heavy wood door.

The knob turned with a squeak and the door opened, revealing a breath-taking troublemaker in jeans and a grey hoodie, his backpack strap over his left shoulder and hands in his pockets. His brown hair was short and cut at odd angles, but for some reason, it didn't subtract from his looks, it added to it, giving him a wild-child air. He stepped into the room, his gold eyes surveying the area for an empty chair so that he wouldn't have to stand at the front of the class and introduce himself.

The New Kid.

His eyes fell over my table and continued on, his face falling into despair.

A spark of anger ignited inside my chest—it was like spilling Tabasco sauce into a paper cut—he was one of *those* guys who were "too cool" to sit next to me. I flashed a look at Jenny, but she hadn't seemed to notice the disturbance.

"Excuse me," the New Kid said awkwardly. "Is this Chemistry with Mr. Turner?"

The grey-haired teacher nodded his head and gestured for him to walk in. "Yes, it is. You must be Mr. Harper. Come in and take a seat next to Miss Blake." He pointed to me.

Harper stood there for a moment, not moving, contemplating his next words. "Doesn't she already have a partner?" he asked innocently.

Everyone's head turned to see how I'd react, knowing that Jenny had been my partner.

I looked at Jenny—who finally noticed Harper and began humming "Forget You" by Ceelo Green—and took a deep breath. This was not going to be fun. Looking straight at Harper and forcing a smile, I replied, "I had a partner, Jenny, but she died in a car accident a couple days ago."

All heads turned to see Harper's reaction now; they kind of reminded me of spectators at a hockey game waiting for one of us to throw the first punch.

He nodded his head as if he'd expected this reply, then silently walked over and gingerly took the seat next to me.

Jenny did not appreciate getting sat in; in a flash, she stood by my side. "Mimi! He took my spot!" she cried out furiously.

"It's not your spot," I said under my breath, causing Harper to turn and look at me.

"What was that?" His gold eyes seared into the side of my skull.

"Nothing. I wasn't talking to you," I hissed and went back to my notes. I glanced over to see if he was still glaring at me, but his attention had shifted to Jenny. It was as if he was staring at her, like he could see her, and that's why he hadn't sat down next to me.

I threw the thought away; he couldn't see her. Nobody but me could see her nor would anyone else ever see her. I was the loner here.

Or so I thought.

The class continued on, and Harper didn't say another word to me until we were halfway through the experiment. "Mimi, what are we doing exactly?" he asked, holding up the piece of magnesium with his tweezers.

"We're seeing how chemical reactions change the properties of elements by taking magnesium and oxygen and forming magnesium oxide by heating the strip of magnesium," I explained in an annoyed manner, still angry from earlier.

"And we're doing this because?" He tried to keep the conversation alive, but I glared at him.

"Because it's what we're expected to do," I snapped. Then I struck the match against the matchbook and lit the Bunsen burner.

"You don't like me," he continued on, not intimidated by my cold actions towards him, "and I understand why, but I didn't know about your friend."

"Heat it," I commanded, and he looked at me with confusion. "We need to heat the magnesium," I elaborated for him.

He cocked his head slightly then shrugged. He began to put the magnesium in the flame, and I blew out the burner. "What was that for?" he protested.

"Are you stupid? Didn't you read the instructions at all?" I took the magnesium from him and put it in the ceramic dish.

"But you said—"

"—to heat it, not to put it directly in the flame! You almost ruined the experiment." I relit the burner and placed it under the heating stand.

Harper put the ceramic dish with the magnesium on the stand and said nothing.

"Hmph." I shook my head and waited while the magnesium heated up. As I watched the clock, a sudden thought hit me; how had Harper known my name? I'd never mentioned it, and Mr. Turner only referred to me by my last name, so how had he known my first? I glanced at him and tried to remember if anyone else had mentioned it during class.

"How long until somebody screws up?" Jenny asked me with a yawn of boredom.

"Not long now," I replied, knowing that if anyone were to hear me, they would think I was referring to the experiment.

"Ugggh! That's far too long, I'm bored," she moaned. She glowered at Harper who had his back to us. "You know, for as super-hot as he is, he's kind of a dick."

I nodded my head in agreement. Harper looked over his shoulder at me and I wondered whether he had heard Jenny's comment. Jenny had said my name earlier and he hadn't reacted at all—Jenny had said my name.

He flashed an amused smile at Jenny for a split second before he turned his head back towards the experiment. My heart began to race; he could see Jenny! How else could he have known my name when nobody else had said it?

"I think the magnesium is reacting with the oxygen." Harper pointed out as I continued to stare at him. "Mimi?" He turned his head again and I could see it in his eyes; he knew I had found him out. It amused him.

I wasn't going to let him get any enjoyment out of it. "Ya think?" My voice was like acid even in my own ears.

He blew out the burner, picked up his lab book, and began scribbling down observations.

I walked over to the experiment and glanced into the dish; the magnesium was now white magnesium oxide.

"You're good at what you do," he said lightly, still looking down at his lab book.

I knew he wasn't talking about the lab. "You have no idea."

"Try me." He put the lab book down.

He wanted me to say something, he wanted me to admit that Jenny was standing in the classroom with us. He wanted me to say another word. He wanted me to acknowledge that he knew my secret. But I remained silent and began to pick up the experiment.

He took a deep breath and sighed. I guess he knew I wasn't about to talk to him, nor would I ever choose to talk to him about this. Giving up, he helped sponge down the equipment and by the time we finished, the bell rang.

I was out of there like a bat out of hell; just being near Harper sent chills down my spine. Something about how he knew, or at least how he acted like he knew, it made me feel threatened. Even his smile was like a dagger in my back, it screamed "I know your secret" and it killed me having this kid, who I didn't even know, be able to ruin my life with one word.

I rounded the corner and crashed into Charlie. "Sorry!" I apologized, kneeling to help pick up the scattered textbooks that he'd been carrying.

"No problem, I like it when my books go flying," he replied with a smile.

"Sorry," I repeated, returning the smile. I felt relieved to see him in a better mood.

"So how is it you managed to crash into me in broad daylight in a nearly empty hallway?" Charlie asked once he'd gotten all his books off the floor.

I looked behind me to make sure that Harper kid hadn't followed. "I was running from that New Kid."

Charlie raised his brow. "The New Kid?" he repeated.

I gave him my personal death stare. "I had to sit next to him in Chemistry and he was all . . . ." I shivered and Charlie began to laugh. "What's so funny?"

"Is he really that ugly?" Charlie answered, catching his breath.

I took a step back. "No! He's insanely hot!"

"Then what's the problem?" Charlie opened his locker and threw his books inside. He seemingly flinched at the thundering of his books crashing onto the metal bottom of the locker, but that could have been my imagination. The sound echoed through the halls and back before he turned to look back at me.

My mouth opened and closed but no words came out. Charlie didn't know about it, there was no way he could understand. I had to be quick. "He walked into class and made a huge ordeal about where he should sit and the only open chair . . . ."

". . . Jenny's." Charlie's smile disappeared and he kicked the locker close. "I understand."

I bit my lip; I hated lying to him about all of this, but I couldn't bring myself to burden him with the truth. "She hasn't been gone that long."

Charlie blinked back tears. "You know, sometimes I think I hear her and her stupid comments on everything, complaining to us about school and everything else."

"Me too." I put my hand on his arm to comfort him.

"I just wish I could've said goodbye. I feel so horrible about how the last thing I said to her was 'go to hell' and then she—" He hit the locker with his fist.

"It's not your fault she's dead, Charlie. It was a horrible accident, but that's what it was, an accident." I consoled him.

He shook his head with shame. "No, I'm her boyfriend, if I had just agreed to go with her, she'd still be here."

"Or you'd both be dead." I dropped my hand and looked away. Neither of us dared to admit it, but we both knew it was true. Had either of us joined her, we'd also be dead.

"It should have been me, not her," Charlie spat angrily. "She had dreams and a bright future, and it was all cut short because of that stupid car!"

I sniffed and sank to the floor. "We shouldn't have come today; we're not ready for school."

Charlie sat down next to me and put his arm around me, he could tell everything he said upset me more. "No, she would have wanted us to continue on without her, she'd want us to move on."

I took a shattered breath and buried my eyes into my knees. "I hate this! I hate all of it! Nobody will even talk to us, and even Teddy skipped the funeral; he hasn't talked to me since I told him. I just want things to go back to how they were!" I could feel the tears soak through the fabric of my jeans.

"Teddy's an abusive jerk, Jenny always told you that. You're better off without him," Charlie said softly.

"It doesn't make me feel any better. Who breaks-up with a girl the same day her best friend is pronounced dead?!" I cried even harder. I was glad that the hallway was deserted.

"Jackasses, Jocks, and soulless bastards; Teddy's all of the above," Charlie said gravely, and I laughed slightly.

"You're right. I am better off without him." I lifted my head; the tears were still falling, but I was sure that most of the makeup had rubbed onto the fabric of my jeans.

Charlie let out a mock gasp. "She agreed with me on something!"

I laughed. "Don't get used to it, it will never happen again." I wiped the tears away and took a deep breath. "I'm going to work," I told him, pushing myself to my feet.

"Why would you ever want to go back to work, especially now?" Charlie wondered aloud as I pulled him to his feet.

"Because if I can't be consoled, I might as well try to help someone who can be," I explained with a sad smile. "You can come if you want."

Charlie shook his head. "The funeral home is the last place I want to be right now."

"Suit yourself. I'll see you later, Charlie."

"See ya." He waved and I began to walk down the deserted hall.

I took the precaution to make sure that he was gone before I began to talk to Jenny. It wasn't like anyone else was around, they were all at sports practice or home; no one would care if I talked to the dead for a little bit.

But where was Jenny?

"Jenny?" I called down the empty hallways, my voice bouncing off the floor and red lockers. "Jenny, where are you?" I'd just been with her in Chemistry, it's not like she could have gone that far. I decided I might as well head towards the chem-lab room just to make sure she wasn't trying to mess with the equipment.

An image of the chem-lab room on fire flashed across my mind; Jenny in a room with a bunch of chemicals that could explode? I quickened my pace.

I rounded a corner and got the sudden feeling of eyes burning into my back. I spun around and found nothing but the deserted hall of the school. But the feeling was still there. I took a deep breath. "I'm emotionally distraught," I told myself, "there is nothing here, nobody is watching me; I need to relax."

"I wouldn't say nobody's watching you." A voice came from behind me and I spun around again.

The hallway was just as deserted as before. I ran over and looked behind the vending machines, but found it empty as well. Where the heck was this voice coming from?

"Oh, you can't see me, but I'm watching you." The voice came again, and I realized it was coming from above me, not behind.

"Who are you?" I demanded angrily, snapping my head up towards the ceiling.

"The one who takes what he wants then leaves," the voice replied. "But you already knew that."

Nothing above me either! Where the hell was this ghost? "Takes what he wants, huh? You sound a bit like my ex," I said, trying to will myself to see where it was hiding.

The voice laughed. "You laugh now, but you will soon learn." It was a threat.

"Hmm, not really my style," I said with a shrug. "How about this: you tell me who you are, and then I'll help you crossover and we go our separate ways."

"You cannot help crossover one who is already damned," the voice chided.

"Who's to say you're damned?" The hairs on the back of my neck rose. I forced myself to remain calm as the ghost let out another chilling cackle that scratched the air like fingernails on a chalkboard.

"This is a warning, Mortuus Loquis, stay out of my way. The next time we cross paths, it won't be so pleasant."

I snorted. "You call this pleasant, you're too afraid to even show your face!" I said, provoking it; the most dangerous of all my approaches. I had to see what I was dealing with.

A black shadow appeared before me; the shadow of a figure. A pale face materialized, one with crazy yellow eyes and the look of pure evil. I had to force back the scream that had jumped to my throat at its sudden appearance. This was no ghost; this was a demon.

"This is your only warning," it told me with a wicked smile.

Anger boiled up in my chest, how dare it threaten me on my turf?! "Am I supposed to feel threatened by this?" I asked, getting right into its face.

"That is up to you, but if you are wise, you'll listen."

"Too bad, I'm a teenager; there's not a wise bone in me."

Its look was daggers, but I didn't back down. "Very well. You will find no mercy from me."

"And you shall find none in return." I returned the stare and with that, it disappeared in a black cloud. When it was gone, I felt all the bravery desert me; I crumpled to the floor like the scared little kid I was and hugged my knees to my chest. The weight of that conversation crushed down on my heart like a brick on a grape: squish!

"Holy crap, are you brave!" Harper exclaimed, stepping out of his hiding place behind one of the vending machines. His brown hair was messy, and he looked as if he'd just rolled around in a dust pile. "You just stood up to a demon who threatened you? Most people would have cowered in fear." His eyes fell upon me now, all huddled up on the floor. He ran over to me and knelt. "Are you okay?" he asked with concern.

I stared at him as if he was nuts. "What do you think?" I cried out in astonishment. "I just got threatened by a demon and I don't even know what it was talking about, and now I can possibly get killed by doing something that I don't even know about and . . . and where'd you come from?!"

Harper looked down at his clothes, realizing for the first time that they were filthy. "Oh, I was exploring the vents when I heard you calling out for your friend, then, well, you can guess the rest."

I continued to stare at him. "Who are you?"

"Dustin Harold Harper," he replied, holding out his hand for me to shake. "The last living descendant of Michael J. Harper, one of the best Mortuus Loquis this nation has ever known."

"Whoa, whoa, whoa, hold on a second, what is a Mortuus Loquis?" That was the second time I'd heard those words, and I deserved an explanation.

"It's Latin for 'Dead Speak'," Dustin replied.

"And you're related to other people who can communicate with the dead?" At this point, my mind was on the verge of exploding and sending pieces of brain all over the walls.

"Uh, duh." He laughed but stopped when I didn't join in. "So, is it your mom or your dad who has the sight?"

"Neither. I'm so confused." I put my hands to my head to keep it from spinning.

"Wait, you don't know whether your parents can see ghosts or not?" Dustin was appalled at this.

"Of course, they can't! They're as normal as normal can be! I'm the only odd ball here, I didn't even know there were other people who could see ghosts and . . . I think I'm going to puke."

Dustin backed away a little and looked around. "Come with me, this isn't the place to dwell and have a chat."

"I don't want to go anywhere with you," I finally admitted. "I would rather sit here."

"Well, that isn't an option at this point, Mimi, so please." He held out his hand. "I can always carry you if you refuse."

"Then you'll just have to carry me." I doubted he would go through with his threat.

Dustin shrugged. "Alright, but I did give you the choice." He leaned down, scooped me up into his arms, and started walking down the hallway.

"What the hell are you doing?!" I screamed.

"Carrying you," he replied.

"Put me down!"

"Nope."

"PUT ME DOWN!" I screamed in his ear, but he just ignored me. Alright, time to try a different angle. "Please put me back down on the ground. I need to find Jenny."

A guilty look crossed Dustin's face. "About that."

"What did you do to her?!" My voice cracked with fear.

He pulled out an antique locket and showed it to me. It was gold with a floral design around the edges, and it was strung upon a gold chain. "I trapped her in here."

I grabbed at the locket, but he pulled it away. "That's my best friend you've got in that thing!"

Suddenly, he dropped me, and I landed on my tailbone. I let out a cry of pain and glared up at him.

"This is my leverage," he said, dangling the locket above my head. "If you want your friend back, then you have to earn her back."

"You jerk! What kind of a deal is that?!" I was pissed that he would even think of committing such a heinous act of . . . whatever this would be considered. Kidnapping— ghostnapping—whatever!

"It's the only one you've got." He pocketed the chain then smiled at me. "So, are you willing to lend me an ear and find out what that demon is up to, or are you going to sit there, dawdling in confusion?"

I glared at him; he really did not think all that highly of me. He thought I was incompetent to everything! What a jerk. But I had to get Jenny back; even she didn't deserve eternity in a locket.

Pushing myself to my feet, I smacked the dust off my clothes and took a deep breath. "You're a real ass. If you wanted to be my friend that badly, then you should have chosen a different method of attack that didn't involve attacking me physically. I'll listen to what you have to say, but I will do no more."

"Fine, then you'll never see Jenny again. I'll just drop her down a street drain on the side of the road." He began to walk away.

My fists clenched in anger, what was with this guy? Why did he want me to listen to him so badly? I bit my lip; I was going to have to do as he said, for now at least, just until I could steal the locket off his person. "Wait," I said reluctantly.

Dustin turned around and smiled at me, his gold eyes shining. Oh, how I loathed him. "What was that? Did I hear you give up?"

"No, I'll do what you want, but that does not make us friends," I said coldly.

"Perhaps not, but I wouldn't doubt the possibility," he said and began to walk off again.

"Damn him," I cursed under my breath.

CHAPTER THREE:

So, you know how your parents used to warn you not to step into a car with some random stranger when you were little? Well, I missed that talk. In my town, everybody knew everybody, so you'd never have to worry about your kids getting kidnapped or lost because it just didn't happen.

Dustin, however, had grown up on the streets of Chicago, where everyone is a stranger and likely to mug you . . . which was also why he was so rude.

We came from two separate worlds.

I followed him out to the parking lot. I should have expected it to be so late; dealing with the supernatural, especially with demons and other apparitions of the like, tends to bend time into the spirit dimension. But that didn't stop me from being surprised that most of the kids were already getting out of sports practice and heading to their cars or waiting for their ride home.

And they were all staring at us.

In a small town like mine, there is hardly anything to gossip about so everything is fair game. Heads turned as Dustin walked out of the doors, shortly followed by me. Dustin was already a topic of gossip, being the new kid and all, but throwing me on top of it only added to it. I could hear their thoughts in my head; "Why is he covered in dust? Are those two dating? Isn't she dating Teddy? What a freak. I'm going to call the entire student body!" The voices overflowed my brain while their gazes burned my skin, leaving marks.

Despite all the eyes, Dustin didn't seem to notice. Maybe he was used to people judging him wherever he went, or maybe he just could care less, but I thought I was going to die.

"Dustin, where are we going?" I asked quietly.

He looked over his shoulder at me and smiled. "This place I found; you'll like it there."

A shiver slid down my spine, leaving me with a sinister idea of what he meant by that. "How long did you say you've been living here?"

"I didn't." Dustin stopped before the old silver Cadillac De Vil and unlocked the doors. He opened the passenger side door and gestured for me to step in. Reluctantly, I did, and he closed the door.

"I know I should have asked this before, but are you planning on killing me?" I asked when he stepped into the driver's seat.

Dustin laughed. "If I wanted to kill you, I wouldn't have let myself be seen leaving with you before the majority of the student body, now would I?" He gunned the engine and it roared to life.

"You could be a real stupid killer." I countered. I blushed at his failed attempted to lift his eyebrows.

"I'm not a killer," he assured me, pulling out of the parking spot. "I may be able to talk to the dead, but I sure as hell don't make 'em that way."

"I still don't trust you."

"But yet you stepped into a car with me."

"I was forced to step into a car with you."

Dustin laughed again and shook his head. "Choices: would you jump off a bridge if Jenny did? I sure as hell wouldn't because it's the choice that counts. Whether or not you believe it, you have the choice to step into situations, and you can always choose to tuck and roll out of the vehicle you stepped into."

"I'd prefer to not get road-burn." I crossed my arms and looked out the window.

Dustin sighed and pulled over just on the edge of the parking lot. "You can leave right now; I won't force you to come with."

I glared at him. "I made my decision, and I don't change my mind easily."

"Alright." He began driving once more and remained silent as he drove.

We drove about five minutes before I realized he was driving towards the cemetery. He turned through the third wrought-iron gate and down the short path, stopping next to the chapel.

"You brought me to the cemetery?" I asked. "Maybe you are a smarter killer than I first assumed. Burying a body with all the rest—nobody would ever know."

"If you thought I was a killer, why would you tell me that?" Dustin shook his head, stepping out of the car and into the fading twilight.

"It's a way of coping with unpredictable situations," I replied, taking a deep breath and holding it for a few seconds before exhaling. "See, coping."

"Well can you cope on the go? I don't want an audience." He looked around as if anyone was there in the deserted cemetery with us, and then quickly hopped up the steps of the chapel.

"Dustin, just stop. I've already been in the chapel countless times, there's nothing special about it."

"It's not the chapel itself that is so interesting; it's what's beneath the chapel that I want to show you."

"But there isn't anything under the chapel," I countered, following him inside. The chapel is a small building built with a square floorplan. It's too small for anything other than the gray granite altar and large crucifix that hung from the wooden rafters.

"And that's where you are so wrong, Mimi," he said with a smile as he walked over to the small altar.

I rolled my eyes, closed the huge oak door, and genuflected.

Dustin gave me a confused look. "What are you doing?"

"I'm showing my respect to the Big Guy," I replied, doing the sign of the cross, followed by pointing at the crucifix hanging before the wall.

"You believe in that?"

"Don't you?"

He shook his head.

Again, I rolled my eyes. "You can accept demons and ghosts, but not the God who created all life? Typical."

"Typical?" Dustin cried out indignantly. "How is there anything 'typical' about me?"

"You can look no further than what is before you. That's what," I replied heatedly. "And then you wonder why people don't trust you."

He snorted and began pushing on the stone altar. "The only one who doesn't look at what's before her is you, sweetheart."

I growled; did he just call me "sweetheart"? "What is that supposed to mean?"

He grunted as the altar began to move, revealing a small opening in the floor with steps leading downwards. "I bet you never would have discovered this if not for me." He rubbed his hands together and gestured towards the steps, awaiting my response. "After you, sweetheart."

I felt my cheeks flush. That ignorant little jerk! No one, and I mean no one, has the right to talk to me like that!

I remained where I stood.

He shrugged, then began to climb down the steps. "Alright then."

I stared at the alter in disgust; not only did he insult me, but he desecrated a holy object while doing so. Who did this guy think he was?

Dustin popped his head out from the floor. "Are you coming or not?" And with that, he disappeared once again into the ground.

I stood up there alone in the empty chapel, trying to decide whether it would be worth it to follow the guy I'd just met into the crypt that shouldn't have existed. Reason told me "no."

Screw reason! That's what got me into this mess in the first place. I looked down at my watch and took a deep breath of musty air. Ten minutes, that's all he had.

And with that, I followed Dustin down the granite steps and into the crypt under the chapel.

The air became damp and cold as I descended the steps after Dustin, and what little light had streamed in from the stained-glass windows of the chapel was snuffed out after the first curve. My heartrate climbed as I stumbled down, deeper and deeper into the unknown. There were a few moments in which I was tempted to run back, to leave Dustin down there alone, but then I would remember Jenny and I knew that I was doing this for her.

After what felt like an eternity, I saw a light at the bottom of the cold, dark steps. I stopped on the edge of the light; was it safe to continue and join Dustin, or was this a trap of some kind, like in the movies? I smiled inwardly; if this was a movie, I'd already be dead.

Stepping into the light, shading my eyes as they readjusted from the pitch blackness of the steps, I saw a large library.

No joke, an actual library was under the cemetery.

My jaw dropped as comprehension began to kick in; there was a library, an ancient and musty library, under the cemetery.

Dustin had climbed one of the hardened maple ladders on a moveable line that was connected to the classic oak shelves and was pulling down one of the heavy, leather-bound tomes. He dropped it on one of many tables which were scattered about the endless rows of books, sending dust flying in all directions. He looked up and smiled at my amazement. "I told you you'd be amazed." He sat down on a stool with a smug look on his face.

"This is extraordinary!" I gaped at the impossible size, it had to be at least the length of two football fields, if not longer, and wide and open like the library of congress. I looked up and saw a mural of the night sky, the galaxies and planets included. It was the most beautiful room I'd ever seen in my life.

"And to think, you thought I was bringing you here for murder," He puffed impatiently, gesturing for me to come join him.

"This can't be real." My mind was fuzzy, this couldn't possibly be real, it was too remarkable, too mind-boggling; words can't accurately describe the impossibility of that room. "It's just too unbelievable."

"So are ghosts and life after death, but we both know that they exist," Dustin remarked, tapping his foot impatiently.

I shook my head and took a deep breath. "All this time, this place has been under the cemetery and nobody has ever discovered it." I began to make my way towards Dustin.

"I wouldn't say 'nobody,'" Dustin said slowly.

"What do you mean?"

"We discovered it."

"You did, I just came with you."

"And it had to be built by someone and taken care of. If you haven't noticed, the room is well preserved, even the books are, see? Someone fixed the binding on this recently." He lifted the book to show me. "So, someone else must know of this place."

Light bulb. "You want me to sit down here and wait to see if whoever it is shows up, don't you?" That was the absolute last thing I wanted to do with my Friday night.

Dustin smiled, revealing two rows of perfect, sparkling white teeth. "I knew you were useful."

"I am not going to spend my Friday night down in some creepy crypt under a cemetery," I told him outraged.

"You are actually," he said with certainty. "Out of your own free will too."

"Oh really, and what makes you so sure that I will want to stay?" I snapped.

He leaned back on his stool, somehow managing to stay balanced. "Mimi, despite your act, I know you're just as curious as I am as to what the meaning of all this," he gestured to the room around him, "is. And I'm quite sure that if we can get to the bottom of this, then we can get some answers about the demon and why it was threatening you."

I hated knowing that he was right. I hated everything about him, and yet, there was something about him that was just so enthralling, so different. He was the only one who cared, who cared about me, and in spite of my profound intolerance of him, he still wanted to make sure I was going to be safe. At the time, I found it annoying as hell. Now, I realize just how lucky I was that he'd resolved to help me.

Stomping my foot in defeat, I took a seat next to Dustin, who just continued to smile contently. I glanced down at my watch and felt my heart drop; it had already been half an hour since I'd decided to descend the steps. I wouldn't be going any time soon.

We sat there in silence for a while longer, but soon I grew restless and bored. "What's with the book?" I gave in to my curiosity.

Dustin opened an eye slightly. "What book?" he asked innocently.

"The one you put on the table, nitwit." I scowled angrily.

He yawned and looked at the table with fake surprise. "Oh, you mean *that* book."

I clenched my fist but forced myself to relax, figuring that Dustin enjoyed seeing me wound up. "Yes, that book," I said through my teeth.

Dustin smirked and lazily began to flip through the pages. "This is the fifth tome of the Demonology section on the wall. I figure your friend will be in it."

I leaned in closer to get a better look at the book. The pages were yellowed with age, and the quality of the paper was poor. I caught a few words as Dustin flipped the pages, but they were undecipherable, most likely in another language.

"Latin," Dustin said, reading my thoughts. "This one is in Latin, written around the same time as Julius Caesar's assassination; 'Et tu, Brute?'"

"How'd ya know that?" I gave up trying to keep the curiosity from my voice.

"I don't, I just made it up for show," he replied simply.

I punched his arm.

"Ow! What was that for?" he cried, rubbing his arm where the purple and black bruise began forming.

"What, are you gonna cry?" I taunted.

"I always could . . . would it make you feel bad?" He winked a golden eye at me.

"Not at all," I replied, pulling my long black hair back to begin braiding it.

"That's too bad; I was hoping you were more of a softy." He returned to flipping through the pages covered in Latin.

I stood up, not wanting to deal with him, and began browsing the endless isles of books. There were so many, all the way from Plato's *Republic* to theories on evolution. Demonology was only a small portion of the library. Thousands of smaller books on things I'd never heard of were there. Religions, science, civilizations, mathematics, language, even fiction. The rows of books ordered by section seemed to continue forever.

My legs walked down the aisles, led by my eyes, looking for something to catch them. Never in my life have I seen so many books in one place, all in working condition, some older than time itself. The voice in my head kept telling me that all books, all written words, were here in this library. I could wander for years and still never see them all.

A book caught my eye: it was on the edge of a shelf, not put away, as if someone didn't feel the need to put it in its rightful place. I picked it up and examined it. It looked old—not quite as old as most of the books in the room—at least 18th or 19th century old. I couldn't find a title, but it didn't seem to need one.

Looking around to see if anyone else was there, I carefully opened the book and began skimming the pages. To my surprise, they were all handwritten, not typed. At the bottom of the first page, I was able to make out the words:

This is the property of Charlemagne the Immortal Protector.

I stared at the letters on the book; the handwriting looked like Charlie's. I shrugged it off. A lot of people have similar handwriting, there can only be so much variation.

Besides, Charlie is only a little older than I am. There's no way he was alive whenever this book was written.

I placed the book back on the shelf then slowly meandered back to where Dustin sat, still staring at the Latin pages.

"You were gone quite a while. Find anything interesting?" he asked, not bothering to look up from the pages.

"I'm not sure how, but it seems every book in existence has found its way here."

"Hmmm."

I fell back onto the stool next to him and stared at the book he was reading once more. "You can read Latin?"

"Yeah, ever since I was first learning to read. I can speak it too, even though no one speaks it anymore."

"Why did you learn Latin?"

"Dad thought that it was a useful skill. I can read Latin almost as well as I can read English. Languages are best taught at a young age, so I learned English, Latin, Ancient Greek, German, Spanish, Italian, some Chinese, a bit of Japanese, you know, just enough to get by wherever I end up."

"Do you know Russian?"

"Ya ne govoryu po-russki."

"That's actually kind of cool."

"Mmm hmm."

We sat down in the library for hours as we waited for the mysterious caretaker to come, but he never showed. I fell asleep after a while. Dustin woke me up when he realized that it was pointless to continue.

"Wake up, Mimi." He shook me awake, not bothering to be gentle. "Mimi, I'm going to bring you home."

I lifted my head off the antique wooden table and blinked the sleep out of my eyes. "What time is it?" I asked, trying to stifle a yawn.

"Almost midnight."

I leaped to my feet. "Midnight?!" I cried. "Why didn't you wake me sooner?"

"Y—y—what? W—why are you freaking out?" The look on his face was confusion.

"My parents are going to flip!" I began to run towards the door.

"Mimi, wait!" Dustin charged after me.

"I can't! I'm in so much trouble." I reached the door.

Dustin caught my arm as I began opening the door. "Hold on a second." His voice was soft with . . . concern? "I thought I heard something," he whispered in my ear.

I became quiet and listened hard. Then I heard it too; the patter of footsteps descending the stairs. I quietly slid the door shut and turned to Dustin. "What do we do?" I whispered in panic.

"I don't know, I haven't thought that far!" He joined in with my panic.

I pushed down the urge to smack him and instead pulled him behind a bookcase just as the grand oaken doors began to open.

". . . no, I'm going down there right now. . . I know I haven't been down here in a few weeks, but things have been out of hand lately, so I haven't had the chance." It was Charlie. His red hair shone in the artificial light and he wasn't wearing his glasses.

"It's Charlie!" I exclaimed quietly.

"Who's Charlie?" Dustin wondered.

"My best friend. How does he know about this place?"

"Did ya text him?"

"No, he thinks I'm at work. He doesn't even know about how I can communicate with the dead!"

Dustin raised his brows. "How is he your best friend if he doesn't even know the truth about you?"

"It's complicated," I replied.

Charlie was talking on his cell phone as he walked through the library. "It's not that I wanted to desert my job, it's just that there was a crisis and I had to be there for my friend." Pause. "My girlfriend died. Cut me some slack, I'll dust tonight and—I have to call you back." He hung up and stared at the book that Dustin had neglected to put away.

"Ah crap! I knew I should have put that back on the shelf!" Dustin swore under his breath.

"I thought you wanted to meet the caretaker."

"I wanted to see him, not exactly meet him." Dustin ducked down as Charlie looked over our way.

"Well what are we supposed to do?" I squeaked.

"Who's there?" Charlie asked. "I know someone is here. Who are you?" He slowly backed towards one of the adjacent bookshelves and reached behind one of the books for . . . oh crap! A dagger!

I grabbed Dustin's arm. "What do we do?"

"This!" Dustin threw me out from behind the bookcase.

I screamed as the dagger flew past my ear, sinking into the wood of the bookcase next to my head. "CHARLIE! IT'S ME!" I dove as another blade brushed past me, nicking my arm.

"Matilda?" Charlie questioned, picking up another blade from behind the books.

"Yes! It's me! Would you quit throwing knives at me!?" I watched as he contemplated what I said. Hope began to blossom in my chest, maybe Charlie wouldn't kill me.

"That isn't enough." He pulled his arm back to throw the next knife at me and I dove under a table.

Thunk! The blade sunk into the leg of the table and I let out another scream and crawled out.

Charlie grabbed my hair and yanked me to my feet, pushing the tip of his last knife against my throat. "One more move, and I'll cut your cursed throat." His voice was dangerous, and I knew he wasn't kidding.

"Charlie, please! Don't kill me," I begged, tears streaming from my eyes in terror.

He pushed the tip of the knife a little more, drawing blood from my neck. "Silence demon! You will find no mercy from me!"

"LET HER GO!" Dustin shouted across the room. He had managed to pry one of the knives from the bookshelf and was now holding it, ready to throw.

The pressure on my neck receded a little as Charlie turned to look at Dustin, his blue eyes burning with hatred. "And who are you, another one out to kill me?"

"I am no demon, and," he held tighter to the dagger as he aimed, "I can prove it, Jesus bro!"

"How do I know she isn't a demon then?" Charlie demanded.

Part of me was a little shocked that Charlie just accepted the fact that Dustin wasn't a demon, but still thought I was. Why would he just trust what Dustin said but not me?

"If you don't let her go, I will throw this dagger into your skull, and it will hit its mark," Dustin replied dangerously.

"You're not that good a mark."

"Look me in the eyes and tell me that." Dustin stared into his eyes.

I looked myself and I knew that he could kill Charlie if he wanted to. "Don't you dare kill him!" I cried. "If you hurt him, I'll kill you myself!"

That was all the proof Charlie needed. He dropped the knife in horror. "Mimi, it is you!"

"OF COURSE IT'S ME YOU IDIOT!" I screamed at him, and then I hugged him. "Charlie, I'm so sorry that I made you do that!"

Charlie hugged me back. "Mimi, I—I don't know what to say."

"May I suggest we have an explanation as to what you were thinking?" Dustin interrupted. "You did try to kill us."

Charlie let go and stood up straight. "Alright. Right after you explain what the two of you are doing down in my library."

"Your library?" I asked.

"Yes, my library." Charlie puffed out his chest proudly. "I was charged with looking after it, making it my library."

I looked at Dustin and he once again failed to raise only one eyebrow.

I shrugged. "Dustin was showing me this place, saying that it was a safe place to talk."

"To talk about what?" Charlie demanded.

"A demon. Most likely the same one you accused her of being," Dustin replied acidly.

Charlie looked at me with horror. "Are you okay? Did it hurt you?"

I backed away from him and towards Dustin. "Yes, I'm fine," I replied uneasily.

"Jeez, Mimi, you could have been killed!"

"You don't think I know that?" My voice cracked. I felt nauseated and afraid and dizzy. I grabbed the edge of the table, trying to steady myself. Charlie reached out to help, but I swatted away his hand. I was still kind of pissed he didn't trust me, but he trusted Dustin.

The library began to spin around me like a disk and my knees began to wobble, then darkness filled my vision.

I woke up in my own bed, the covers draped over me as if I had fallen asleep there. What the hell happened last night? How did I get home?

"How are you feeling, Mimi?" My dad walked into the room, carrying a tray of breakfast foods in.

"What happened?" My brain was fuzzy.

Dad set the tray down on my bedside table and sat down on my bed. "Charlie brought you home last night. You two had been studying and catching up on homework when you passed out. He says that yesterday was too much for you to handle."

Charlie lied to my dad, which is so unlike him.

I reached up to my neck and found the place where the dagger had pierced my skin. It was covered with dry blood now.

Seeing me touch the wound, dad laughed. "That's what you get for passing out on a pencil. You need to be more careful about where you fall."

I pretended to laugh along. "Yeah, don't I? I'm just lucky it didn't go deeper." I pulled the tray off the nightstand and began to dig in.

"Take it easy, Mimi, I don't want you to overexert yourself for a couple days." He began to tug at his shirt.

"You're grounding me for fainting, aren't you?" I realized, pushing away the tray. "Dad, I was dehydrated, I just need to drink more fluids. I promise you, I'm fine."

Dad sighed. "Just make sure you come to work after school all next week." He stood up and made his way to the door. "Happy Birthday, Matilda." And with that, he closed the door.

CHAPTER FOUR:

I climbed out my second story window and leapt onto the branch of the old maple tree just outside. I had broken my arm multiple times in the past, perfecting this escape route, and now I had it down so well that the tree hardly shakes when I land. I climbed down and looked up at the open window, hoping it wouldn't rain. Shrugging, I snuck out the garden gate and into the neighbor's back yard, out onto the street.

"Took you long enough," Charlie joked as I stepped out onto the street. He was wearing his glasses again and he had changed into jeans and a T-shirt.

"It's my birthday; it's kind of difficult to sneak out," I replied evenly.

Charlie smacked his forehead. "I can't believe I forgot! You're seventeen now!"

I nodded. "And I'm just as old as you now, so don't forget it!"

"Yeah, yeah, sure." Charlie waved it off as if it were nothing. He then became serious. "Mimi, we've got to talk."

"It sounds like you plan on breaking up with me." I smiled to show that I was kidding but he didn't smile in return.

"You can see ghosts."

"And you take care of a library under a cemetery."

"That's different."

"Is it?"

Charlie looked away in frustration.

"I'm still kinda pissed you trusted Dustin but not me." I continued, wanting an explanation.

"He proved he wasn't a demon, you didn't," Charlie replied.

"I don't know where I tuned out, but he never did anything."

"He did. Demon's cannot say holy words, such as the Lord's name. Though he used it in vain, he still spoke Jesus' name."

"It's nice to know that now."

He didn't respond.

"Charlie, I don't know about you, but I kept my secret to protect you," I told him. "Jenny knew and look what happened to her! She's in the ground. It's my fault, Charlie; I never should have told her the truth." I was crying by the end of the speech and sank down onto the cold pavement.

Charlie sank down next to me. "Secrets, that's what killed her," he said bitterly. "She was the only person we told anything, isn't she?"

I sniffed. "Yeah, she was the gossip queen."

"Did she crossover already?" Charlie asked.

I bit my lip.

"Mimi?" His face was full of dread.

"No, she didn't. She's too stubborn to leave," I replied honestly. It was mostly the truth.

"Is she here with us now?"

"Nope, she's in this locket I've got right here," Dustin replied; walking up the street with the locket slung across his chest. He had changed into a clean blue hoody and jeans, and his hair was no longer covered in dirt. I couldn't help but wonder how he knew we'd be here at this precise moment. Maybe he had accompanied Charlie in bringing me home last night . . . or he'd just followed Charlie when he brought me home last night. Great. Not only did I have a dead stalker, I had a living one as well. "I figured that Mimi would be a little reluctant to tell you that one, considering she kept so much from you."

I watched as Charlie's fists clenched and his knuckles turned white.

Dustin also watched it and tossed the locket to Charlie. "Whoa there, tough guy! No need to beat the crap out of me just yet. The locket shebang was all to get Mimi to accept the world she has now been introduced to. You can let your friend out."

"How did you–?" I began, but Dustin cut me off.

"I followed Charlie from a distance, then I heard my name, so I figured you were summoning me so–yeah, how's your day going?"

I rolled my eyes and shook my head.

Charlie also chose to ignore Dustin and opened the locket. We watched as Jenny materialized.

"Thank God!" she exclaimed as she began to stretch her essence. "Do you know how cramped a locket is? If I ever find the guy who locked me in there, I am going to terrorize him until the day he commits suicide."

Dustin smiled and stepped up behind her. "I hope you realize that I have more where that came from," he said quietly in her ear.

Jenny jumped and punched him through the nose.

"You're the a-hole who sucked me up into that locket!"

"Dustin Harold Harper," he replied matter-of-factly. "And I am willing to do it again."

"Ooo you're a real jerk." She breathed and turned to me. "And now you're hanging out with him. You sure know how to pick 'em, Meems."

I took the locket from Charlie. "Do ya wanna go back in here?"

Jenny took a step back. "I am not your puppy! I will not let you treat me like one!"

"Then shut up."

"What is she saying?" asked Charlie, who had only heard half the conversation.

"Nothing dear, Mimi is just being a lunatic," Jenny replied, but Charlie didn't hear.

"Jenny is just being her annoying self," I replied, and Charlie nodded.

"Even in death she has to have the last word." He smiled at the thought.

"I'm going to guess that you two have finally told each other about yourselves," Jenny said casually, looking for a slight hint of gossip.

Dustin was the one to reply. "Yes, and all it took was a knife to her throat and she sang like a canary."

Jenny threw him a loathing look. "You're a monster."

"He wasn't the one holding the knife," I said.

"I was the one holding the knife," Charlie admitted shamefully. "I thought Mimi was a demon."

Jenny looked at Charlie and then to me. "Is that true?"

I nodded and Jenny shook her head. "Wow, this is what happens when I'm gone, you two go all psycho on each other."

"Don't flatter yourself, it would have happened anyways," I said sourly.

"OOOO! Story time!" Jenny sat down on the ground, waiting for an explanation.

I gave it to her. I told her all about the demon's threat and how Dustin dragged me down to the library. Also, about how Charlie nearly killed me.

"And that's why I need to stay here to protect you!" Jenny proclaimed. "Otherwise you'd die."

"I would like to say that I was the one to save her life last night, not you," Dustin said coldly.

"And you were also the one to throw me into the danger," I pointed out.

"He would have found us both. Besides, I wasn't about to let you die."

"No, just get mutilated by my best friend."

"It wasn't that bad, there was very little blood, and even if he had killed you, it would have been quick."

I felt my head begin to spin; the thought of dying made me sick.

Charlie stood up and made a move towards Dustin, who quickly ducked and rolled towards me. "Whoa there, big guy! You need to relax; both you and Mimi are okay, well, mostly okay. You did cut her arm open . . . and her neck. Which, by the way, how are the stitches holding up on your arm?" he lifted the sleeve of my shirt, his gentle touch running over the four stitches. "Good, the bleeding stopped." He let go of the sleeve and it trickled back down my arm.

"Why do you keep showing up?" Charlie finally demanded through clenched teeth.

Dustin smiled at him. "Just think of me as the ghost that just won't cross over; my reasons are apparent, but not always clear." He directed the answer at Jenny, who glared at him.

"So, what are your apparent reasons?" Charlie asked.

"Anyways, so what are you planning on doing today?" Dustin asked me, ignoring Charlie.

I was surprised at the question. "I don't really know . . . maybe go to—"

"—Nowhere. We aren't going anywhere." Charlie quickly cut me off.

Dustin raised his brows. "Alright. Then I'll just go nowhere . . . with Matilda." He jumped to his feet and pulled me to mine.

"What?"

"Charlie clearly wants some alone time with his girlfriend, and I think we should give it to him." Dustin threw a wink at Charlie and began pulling me down the street.

I looked over my shoulder, hoping that Charlie would come running after me, but watched as he glowered. I bit my lip; I was on my own. "Where are you bringing me?"

"Somewhere a little more private," he replied.

"If it's another cemetery, I'm going to tell you right now that I'm not following."

"It's a good thing that I'm not going to one, then."

"But where are we going?" I pressed.

"You know, surprises are good for you, Matilda," he said, stressing my name as if it were a joke.

"Don't call me Matilda," I snarled. "Nobody calls me Matilda."

"I can't imagine why, it's a beautiful name." He sounded authentic when he said it, but I didn't believe him. I hate my name, there's a reason everyone calls me Mimi.

We rounded a corner and I saw the park open out from behind the rows of cute houses that lined the many, rounding streets. Dustin led me through the gate and back towards the playground that, at the time, was empty. The ground was like a wet, muddy sponge, squishing under our feet and getting mud all over our clothing.

He led me to the bench and sat down. "I'm sorry about last night," he finally said.

I sat down next to him, thinking about how to reply. I wanted to say that it was all "okay", but it wasn't; he threw me into harm's way. Who does that? "Good, you should be."

Dustin smiled. "I'm never going to live that down, am I?"

"Never." I smiled back.

Laughing, Dustin looked around the empty park. "This park reminds me of the one back home where I used to go with my friends."

"You had friends?" It came out a little harsher than I meant it to.

"Yes, I know it may be surprising, but I had many friends." Dustin then became quiet.

"What happened to them?"

"Nothing, we grew apart."

I put my chin in my palms and balanced my elbows on my knee, waiting for him to elaborate.

He sighed. "So, most of them didn't like the weird things that tended to happen around me. A couple moved away. One . . . ." he blinked away the tears that began to form in his golden eyes.

"I'm sorry, I shouldn't have prodded," I apologized.

"No, you would have found out sooner or later. Everyone does." His voice was sour. "I walked into his apartment and found him hanging from the rafter; a note written in his own handwriting about how he was sorry, but he couldn't live anymore was on the desk next to him. He didn't even stick around to explain. It was a confirmed suicide, but his parents couldn't handle it. They blamed me."

"You seem to blame yourself too."

"How can't I?! I should have seen the signs that he was suicidal, I was his best friend! I could have stopped him." He stood up, picked a stone from the ground, and chucked it at the slide. The stone ricocheted off the slide and broke through the roof of a melting snow fort.

I flinched. "I know how you feel."

"I know you do. Why do you think I told you all of this? I don't want you to end up like me, you deserve better than what you choose to put up with."

I was shocked, confused, and a little flattered. The Dustin that showed when everyone else was around I hated, but the Dustin I saw in the park was sweet. I took a liking to the sweet version of Dustin; it was refreshing.

"What, you're going to be silent now? Jeesh, maybe I should quit opening up." And there was the jackass again.

"You know, it's easier to feel sorry for you when you're not being a complete dick," I said, rather flustered.

Dustin raised his brows. "Do you think I want your pity? I want you to learn from my mistakes, to not make the same ones. God, girls are stupid."

And there went the last of my pity. "Fine, I take back everything I said. You don't have friends because you're a jerk and you couldn't be nice to broccoli!" I stood up and felt my cheeks flush with anger. "Stay here. I don't want to see you. I'm not even sure why I let you bring me here in the first place! If you're going to be like—like this, then I don't want to talk to you or even be associated with you!" I began to storm off when Dustin softened up again.

"Mimi, wait!" He ran and grabbed my arm.

I flinched in pain; he grabbed the place where the stitches were.

My flinch didn't go unnoticed by Dustin. He quickly let go of my arm and apologized, saying that he was sorry and other things that are contradictory to each other. Then he freaked when the blood began to soak through my shirt.

"Mimi, I am so sorry!" He was back to sweet Dustin again. "Here, I'll stitch your arm back up, that way your parents won't find out the truth." He led me back to the bench and pulled out a needle and thread.

"Do you normally keep a first aid kit in your pockets?" I asked.

"Always. Band-Aids, athletic tape, needle and thread, and a small bottle of things to dress the wounds. You never know when you're going to need them." Dustin smiled.

"Maybe I should start carrying a first aid kit on me, because at this rate, I'm going to need it more than you." I joked.

"Hmm," he agreed.

"Dustin, why are you really here?" I asked amidst the needle and thread pulling through my arm. "And I don't want some cooked-up answer or riddle. I want the straight up truth."

Dustin finished with the stitches and bit the thread so he could tie it. "You want the truth?" He placed the needle and thread back in a pouch that he placed in his coat pocket.

"Yes."

"You need someone, and I need someone. We both lost someone who was close to us, and we need somebody to fill the gap they left behind. It's why you let me bring you here, and why you haven't run. Face it, Mimi, we need each other."

CHAPTER FIVE:

I decided to invite Dustin to my "surprise" birthday dinner with Charlie and my parents.

I think it went well, other than the glares Charlie gave me when he walked through the doors, and the constant questions I got from my parents. But other than that, I say it was pretty good.

After two months, Dustin and Charlie still hated each other, but they had an understanding that they were both a part of my life, so they'd have to deal with it. My parents no longer thought I was crazy since I quit mentioning Jenny. Teddy still hadn't talked to me. I was okay with it for the first month, but after the second, it was ridiculous. Jenny still refused to crossover, but she had chosen to stay with Charlie more, bursting lights and moving chalk to communicate to him that she was still there. Dustin had managed to keep a low profile at school, avoiding fights and gossip so that most the kids hardly knew he existed, which I was happy about.

I discovered that Dustin wasn't all that bad a guy. He has a crude sense of humor, and says whatever he wants, whether it's rude or not, but I kind of like that about him. He's honest, and that's a trait that's hard to come by. He's a little overly sarcastic, but I got used to it after a little bit. It's almost charming.

Yet, after knowing him for about two months, I realized I didn't know anything about him, other than the little information he offered when we first met. He didn't speak of his past, nor of his family. I didn't even know what his favorite color was. At least I didn't know anything more until the night before I got into a fight (it's a long story).

Dustin and I were walking down the street towards the park where we had our first heart-to-heart. It was mid-May and the wind was still cold, so I was bundled up in my black windbreaker, and Dustin was wearing his favorite grey sweatshirt. We were just talking about school and random things, like friends do, when suddenly, he became silent.

That may not seem out of the ordinary, but Dustin is never silent.

"What's wrong?" I asked after a few minutes of silence.

"Why do you always assume somethings wrong when I'm quiet?" he asked.

"Usually because something is wrong," I replied, giving him a small smile. "So, what's on your mind?"

"It's nothing, really, I was just thinking about where I was at this point in time a year ago." He shrugged it off as if it were nothing, but I could hear the sadness in his tone.

"You're thinking about your friend?"

He nodded. "At this point last year, everything was different. The spring is fine, but I don't like the fall. I don't know what it is about fall but change always seems to come. And not the positive sort of change, the kind that sucker punches you in the gut then steals your wallet."

"Was that when Jacob died?"

Dustin became quiet. "No, it's when my parents died."

I stopped in my tracks. "Your parents are dead?"

"Yes."

"How has this never come up before?"

"I don't like to talk about it. I lost a lot when they died."

We were quiet, just standing in the middle of the sidewalk.

"There's a lot you don't know about me Meems," Dustin finally said after a long silence.

"Clearly." I agreed, not knowing what else to say.

"I lived with Jacob and his family until he–well, they couldn't handle me living there without Jacob, so they contacted my uncle and I was here by the end of the week." His voice was sour as he spoke, as if the memory made him sick.

"I'm sorry Dustin, I didn't know."

"I know you didn't, I didn't want that to weigh you down. Death follows me, it always has. I thought if you knew that, you would run."

I punched him.

"What was that for?" he demanded, grabbing his arm and rubbing it.

"I did run. you ghostnapped my best friend, remember?" I smiled as I said it. The entire scenario made me laugh now, every time I looked back at how angry he made me.

Dustin gave me a sheepish smile. "I guess you're right."

"You guess," I repeated sarcastically.

"Hey, there's no need to go hating me, I'm the one with the emotional trauma, and you're making fun of me!"

"I am not making fun of you; I'm just giving you a little taste of your own medicine."

"It tastes awful, how do you take it?"

I winked at him then looped my arm through his. "It doesn't taste so bad over time."

"Tell that to Charlie."

"I have, he doesn't appreciate it."

We continued walking down the street in the fading twilight.

Dustin looked down at his watch. "It's getting late, I should bring you home."

I rolled my eyes. "You mean you're hungry! That's the only time you suggest it's time to go."

"My uncle told me dinner is at nine, no later. I got in trouble the last time I was late, so I'm not about to let it happen again."

"Alright, I'll let you go home and eat."

He smiled at me, then bid me goodnight.

* * *

The snow was finally gone, and spring was in full swing; flowers were blooming, the grass was green, trees were blooming, the temperature became comfortable, and the birds came back. How I loved the spring, even though

Jenny was complaining about not being able to experience the full thing.

You're probably wondering why I'm fixating on spring. Well, I want to paint a nice picture of the setting for what is going to happen during the last weeks of spring and into early summer. That's when the chaos began.

As usual, spring fever hit everybody; no one wanted to be inside, people were getting sick of each other, fights were breaking out, the usual. The only exception was Dustin. Maybe it was because of his years in Chicago, or maybe because he really could care less, but he never once complained about school.

Okay, so it all boils down to me running into Teddy in the hallway for the first time in two months. He had done his best to avoid this, but it's hard to ignore someone when that person accidentally runs into you while you're talking to your new girlfriend.

That someone was me. Woops.

"Sorry, so sorry I—Teddy?" The awkward level rose at least five measures.

"Matilda, what a surprise." Trust me, he was not thrilled. His golden-brown hair had grown out since I'd last saw him, he'd shaved his stash, and he'd even taken out his piercings so that he looked halfway decent. His face still reminded me of a rat, but other than that, he looked good. And to top that, his Letterman's Jacket was beginning to fit his shoulders.

"Who's this?" I asked, trying to sound casual but utterly failing in all senses of the word.

"This is Trisha, my girlfriend," he replied, pushing the tall blond chick between us.

I nearly gagged as a wave of way too much perfume hit my nose. It wasn't even all one kind either; it was like the chick couldn't decide which perfume to wear so she chose to wear them all, making the air pungent with a hint of confusion in the process. "Hi, nice to," *cough*, "meet you." I choked.

"And you too." She gave me a judging look and it would have ended right there . . . if not for Dustin.

"Mimi! There you are, I've been looking all over for—what's that God-awful smell?!" he exclaimed when he reached me, giving Trisha an accusing glance. "Who's the clown?"

"My name is Trisha," Trisha replied, flushing angrily.

"Cool, but who's the clown?" Dustin repeated himself, pointing back at Teddy.

I wanted to die right there and then. The day had been going bad enough, considering the awkward run-in with Teddy, but adding Dustin on top of it . . . ugh! I wished the earth would have swallowed me up.

Teddy pushed Trisha back and towered over Dustin, staring daggers at him. "What did you say to me, Pal?"

Dustin took a step forwards, not at all intimidated by Teddy's anger and height. "I called you a clown; do you have a problem with that, *Pal*?"

I stepped between them and pushed them apart. "Cool it, here's not the place."

"Get your hands off my boyfriend, bitch!" Trisha shoved me back into one of the lockers.

To hell with no fighting! My temper flared and I acted on impulse. I grabbed her tangled blonde hair and began dragging her, arms flailing and mouth cursing, towards the back doors of the school. The other kids cleared a path; they wanted a fight just as much as I did at that moment. I kicked the doors open and threw Trisha down the steps.

She jumped back to her feet. "I'm gonna kill you for that!" she threatened as I descended the steps.

"Bring it."

She charged at me and I quickly kicked her in the gut. She doubled over and I elbowed her head down to the ground and she smacked onto the pavement. I then put my foot on her spine, applying just enough pressure to hold her there.

Kids came pouring out the doors to watch the fight and were disappointed to find I'd already won. "What was that?" I chided happily.

Someone grabbed my arm; it was Dustin. "What was that about not fighting?"

"She hit me, she won't do it again, and neither will they," I replied amidst the rising disappointment.

"That sure was one hell of a way to do it, you probably should take your foot off her back." He pulled me into the crowd and back into the school.

"What are you doing?" I asked.

"Taking away the evidence. If you're on the other side of the school, you couldn't have been the one to beat up skunky."

"Wow, you do care."

"No, it just gets boring when you're grounded."

"Sure, whatever."

"Miss Blake!" The nasally voice of Vice Principal Teufel yelled.

We stopped dead in our tracks. "Crap." I swore under my breath. Turning around slowly, I forced an innocent look and faced Mrs. Teufel. "Yes ma'am?" I asked as pleasantly as I could manage without gagging.

Mrs. Teufel was an ugly old hag; even her wrinkles had wrinkles. Her crooked nose hung out over the rest of her bony figure and her cold blue eyes were always filled with disgust. Her grey hair was pulled back in a bun on the back of her head and most people joked that she was like that grandmother you never wanted, the one with the axe. "Where do you think you're going?" she demanded.

"Class ma'am," I replied.

"Is that true?" She took a few steps towards us and began stalking around us. "Or are you running from the fight that just happened?" She threw her head around to see my reaction.

I played the "good girl" card. "I didn't want to get involved, so I decided to leave."

She snapped her head to Dustin. "What is your name, boy?" she barked.

"Dustin Harper," Dustin replied automatically.

"Mr. Harper, is this true?"

"Yes ma'am."

She stared us down, but we stared right back. Her eyes narrowed and I forced back the fear of her finding us out. "Alright, get to class!" She snapped at us and we nodded.

"Yes ma'am," we said together and hightailed it out of there.

"Man, what a hag!" Dustin exclaimed once she was no longer in sight.

"I thought she had us for a second." I breathed a sigh of relief. My pulse had quickened through the entire encounter and I only now realized it.

"She was jumping at straws. You sure know how to play your cards right." Dustin raised his brows.

"It's a handy trick," I replied with my eyes shut. "I learned it from watching The Mentalist, Patrick Jane sure knows how to outwit everybody."

"I'm afraid to ask." Dustin smiled.

I punched him. "Don't give me that look! It's a crime show my parents watch!"

"Oh, that's much better, isn't it?"

"What are you two fighting about now?" Charlie asked as he rounded the corner.

"Nothing, we're just celebrating how Mimi escaped detention for kicking someone's butt in a fight," Dustin replied.

Charlie snorted. "Are you hungry?" he asked me.

"Starved. Where's Jenny?" I looked behind him, hoping to catch a glimpse.

"Here!" she exclaimed from the nearby locker. "I was just going through dirt bag's things and you'll never guess what I found."

"I doubt we'd want to guess," Dustin replied and turned to me. "Would you like to finish this conversation later?"

"You mean under less supervision?" I laughed. "Jenny heard the entire conversation already and Charlie could care less. Why don't you just come eat with us?"

Charlie was shaking his head vehemently, but I just ignored him.

"I doubt I'd be welcome." He gestured to Charlie.

"Grow a pair," I replied and hooked my arm through his. "Now, would you both quit acting like children? I have a VP to outrun."

Dustin smiled at this, but Charlie's face turned pale. "You weren't joking about getting into a fight?" He was horrified by the thought.

"Yes, now let's go to Antonio's; I'm craving crinkle cut fries."

We didn't end up going to Antonio's. Somebody ratted me out before we even reached the front doors. I figure it was most likely Teddy because I beat up his new girlfriend or the kid who was being accused, I don't know. Either way, I got pulled into the principal's office and had to wait there for my parents to come. I figure the Principal would have let the matter slide, nobody got seriously injured and it wasn't going to happen again, but Mrs. Teufel couldn't stand the fact that I outsmarted her. The witch had it in for me.

The minutes ticked by while I sat on the uncomfortable wooden bench outside the main office, perfecting my escape route. I could go with the bare truth, but I figured it was already twisted. I came up with some pretty good lies, but I threw them all out. My mind kept falling back on how I was trying to break up a fight and the sudden rage that engulfed me when I was shoved into the lockers. That story was going to get me anger management classes for sure. Maybe the innocent approach—no, I didn't even have a scratch. I could go with the "my best friend died, and some things just set me off" but that would land me with at least two—if not five—months of counseling. I had no time for that.

I would just have to wait and see which one to use.

Tick-tock, tick-tock, tick-tock, the second hand continued to move around the clock face. How long did Principal Bryant say it was going to be? How long had it already been? I focused on the hour and minute hands and found it had only been two minutes. Damn. I found myself thinking that if I ever found the person who ratted me out, I was going to beat them up too. That did nothing to help speed up the clock.

To the on-lookers, I was cool and collective, maybe even slightly rebellious. On the inside, I was freaking out, wondering whether I was going to get expelled or what kind of punishment they had in store. I wanted to run, I wanted to flee, but I had nowhere to go. But I also deserved to be punished; I had broken school rules and gave a girl a bloody nose. Then again, calling my parents was punishment enough.

Mercifully, the clock finally struck four and my parents came walking down the hallway. I looked down shamefully as my parents approached, and I waited for the scolding to begin, but I got an even worse treatment: silence. Nothing is worse than silence. Silence is what happens when you screw up bad, really bad.

Principal Bryant stepped out of his office and he gave me a look of apology. "You may come in now," he said.

Solemnly, I stood up and followed my parents into his office, wishing for the second time that day that I could sink into the ground. I sat down in the center chair while my parents sat on either side, still silent. Mrs. Teufel was hovering over Principal Bryant's shoulder, smirking at me, daring me to plead.

"I believe you were told why you are here, Mr. and Mrs. Blake," Principal Bryant said lightly.

"No, we weren't," Dad replied.

Principal Bryant gave dad a quizzical look. "Aren't you here because Matilda got into a fight?"

The tension left the room at the explanation and my parents began to laugh. I could feel my anxiety melt away. Of course, they thought it was hilarious, considering what they thought it was about.

Mrs. Teufel was startled by their reaction. "This is no laughing matter!" she screeched. "Fights are not authorized on school grounds; this is a serious offense!"

My mom forced back another round of laughter. "Kids will be kids. So long as no one was seriously injured, I'm sure that a week of detention will cut it." She looked at me. "Isn't that right, Matilda?"

I wisely chose not to respond.

"That's settled then, a week of detention, starting next Monday," Principal Bryant agreed.

"Thank you, Paul; it was good seeing you, but next time, let's just go get coffee," Dad told the Principal who heartily agreed.

We left the Principal's office and headed out to the car. I waited for further punishment from my parents, but it never came, so instead I asked. "Aren't you going to ground me?"

"What for?" Mom asked.

"Getting in a fight."

"No, it was a onetime occurrence and you've already punished yourself twofold. Besides, I want to spite that old hag! She told us that you were doing gang-related business."

I burst out laughing. "Even I didn't know I was doing that."

We stepped out of the front doors of school, laughing heartily. The sun was shining, the birds were chirping, everything was good.

I saw Dustin and Charlie sitting on a bench looking with worry up at the school. They jumped to their feet when they saw me and ran over. "Are you okay? What's the verdict? How long are you grounded for?" I don't even know which one said which.

"Guys, chill! I'm fine and I'm not grounded. I've just got detention for the next week."

"Hello Charlie," Dad said with an amused smile.

"Hello Mr. B, Mrs. B. How are you?" he asked, slightly embarrassed he hadn't noticed them before.

"Good, Charlie, you haven't been getting into fights lately, have you?" Mom asked with a smile that Charlie took as an accusation.

"Oh no, ma'am! No fights at all!" Charlie quickly assured them.

Mom winked at me then turned to Dustin. "How are things going for you Dustin?" she asked.

"Pretty Good, Mrs. B, just trying to keep Mimi out of trouble."

"Seems like hard work." Dad raised his brows accusingly at me and I rolled my eyes.

Dustin took that as incentive to humiliate me further. "Don't I know," he threw a quick wink at me, "I slave away, making sure she's alright, and I turn my back for one second, and then she beats a girl up."

"Get over yourself," I said irritably.

"Why don't you boys come over for supper? We're celebrating Mimi not being part of a gang!" Mom said with a chuckle.

"We're celebrating that?" Dad asked. Mom gave him "the look".

"I mean, of course, everybody come and party!"

Charlie gave me a quizzical look.

"Later," I told him.

"Sure, I like food," Dustin replied with a smile.

"I suppose," Charlie replied, reluctant to go anywhere with Dustin.

We all gathered a half an hour later at my house. Dustin rolled up in his Cadi, Charlie hitched a ride with me, and my parents went out and bought "party food" which consisted of Buffalo wings and chips.

While my parents were out getting the food, I took Dustin on a tour of my home. The entrance hall had a winding staircase on each side, giving the house a deceitful appearance of a grand mansion. I led him up the stairs and pointed out my room, my parents' room, the bathrooms, the guest room, and . . . .

"No way! You've got a theater room?" Dustin marveled at the large blank screen laid out across the whole back wall.

"Yeah, don't most people?"

"No! We've got TV rooms, not theater rooms!"

"Is there a difference?"

Dustin looked at me appalled. "Don't you have a TV room?"

"Yeah, this one."

He sighed and sat down on the cushiony couch. "You've got issues, Mimi."

I slid next to him. "How do I have issues!? Doesn't your family have a TV room?"

"That's beyond the point!"

"Is it though?"

"Absolutely."

"Fine. Then your tour stops here. I won't show you the rest of my house." I crossed my arms and leaned back on the couch.

"You're not serious?" Dustin asked.

"I am serious, thank you very much."

"Aww Mimi, I didn't mean to offend you."

"Well you did."

He put his arm around me. "Come on, I'll let you hit on my home when you see it."

"Nope, not going to fall under your peer pressure."

"Please, you know you want to." He leaned in closer.

So did I. "Apologize and maybe, just maybe, I'll forgive you."

"Apologize for what? Being honest?"

"No, for being a jerk."

"I think we both know that's never going to happen."

"Oh really?" Our faces were only inches apart.

"ARE YOU TWO GOING TO KISS?!" Jenny yelled.

I let out a cry of terror and jumped back. Dustin also recoiled in surprise, just not quite as drastically. "God Jenny! You gave me a heart attack!" My heart was pounding a thousand miles per hour and my breathing was hard.

"Should I leave? You two were having a moment there, weren't you?" She winked at me then added in an undertone, "You sure know how to pick 'em."

"No! We were just arguing." I quickly pushed it off. "Weren't we, Dustin?"

"Yeah, at least, I think we were fighting. I still have whiplash from your sudden sensitivity to how much wealth your family has." Dustin sounded dazed.

"Mmm hmm. Go ahead, you two keep telling yourselves that. I know the truth, even if you don't." Jenny assured us.

"There's nothing between us, Jenny," I said sternly, and she turned around.

"Whatever, I'll leave you two to your 'fighting' then." She floated back through the wall.

Dustin turned his attention back to me when he was certain she'd left. "Do you mean everything you said to Jenny?" His voice was casual, but I could feel the weight of his curiosity.

I stood up and walked around the couch. "Don't ask questions you don't want answered."

He stood up as well and came around the other side so that he was facing me. "Who said I didn't want the answer." The light tone from earlier was completely gone.

I turned to face him and saw just how serious he was. His golden eyes no longer shined, his face was stern, and his features were tense. It seemed like he was preparing to get punched.

My mouth opened, but I couldn't find the words. Did I mean what I had said about Dustin and I having no chemistry? We were lab partners in Chemistry, but did we have substance, something to build a relationship with?

Dustin took a few steps towards me and stretched out his hand. "If you tell me there's nothing, there's nothing. If you tell me there's something, there's something. If you're not ready, just tell me, Mimi. I can't keep guessing."

Charlie opened the door, saving me from the horrors of answering his question.

"—Tada! The coin has vanished!" Dustin quickly pretended like he was showing me a lousy magic trick.

"Magic tricks?" Charlie laughed. "And I thought I'd walk in on something more awkward."

"That has been the theme tonight, hasn't it, Mimi?" Dustin smiled at me.

"Uh, yeah, it has." It was my turn to be dazed.

"Wow, I never realized that your mind was so easily dazed," Dustin told me.

"Well, when you throw sudden surprises at me, it takes a little bit for my mind to start working," I replied a little sharper than normal.

"I get the feeling you two aren't talking about magic tricks," Charlie surmised.

"Why do you think that?" Dustin still had his eyes locked with mine. "We're talking about magic tricks, aren't we?"

"Yes, magic tricks." I broke eye contact and turned to Charlie. "Are my folk's home yet?"

"Yup. That's why I came and found you guys." Charlie caught the hint.

"Tell them I'll be down in a minute."

"Alright." He closed the door behind him.

I turned back to Dustin and took a deep breath. "Dustin, I can't deny that we seem to have something, but I just can't handle that right now. I've only been single for two months and I . . . I . . . ."

Dustin closed the distance and put his arms around me. "Hey, I understand. You still have feelings for Dolly—"

"—Teddy."

"Whatever. I told you, I won't make you do anything you don't want to do. I just had to know."

I sniffed and forced back my tears. "I know. I'm really sorry Dustin."

Dustin wiped the escaped tear from my cheek. "It's alright," he said softly. Then, he pulled out the locket from his pocket. "I want you to have this," he said, placing it in my hand.

"Dustin, didn't you give this to Charlie?"

"Yes, but I swiped it back. I found this a while back, and now, I want you to have it."

"Dustin, I can't, really—"

"Please, Mimi, I want you to keep it. Think of it as a promise trinket that I'll be there for you when you need me," he insisted, releasing the grip on my hand.

I smiled at him. "Alright, I'll keep it as a promise."

"Good, now come on, everybody's going to think we're making out," Dustin said, leading me towards the door.

I laughed and felt the rest of my emotions float away. "They already think that."

"True, but I like to break people's expectations."

Okay, so I've kept you waiting for the good part long enough, but I had to share with you all the events that led up to this moment. I had to show you all the people who got involved because not all of them make it out of the catalyst.

CHAPTER SIX:

Charlie, Jenny, Dustin, and I all went to Bagels Are Us the next morning for Cappuccinos and, of course, bagels. The little café is on the corner of Main Street, with the parking lot back through the alley.

We walked through the doors and into the already long line of high schoolers who were also buying breakfast before school began. I reached the counter and ordered my usual plain bagel and strawberry cream cheese. "Would you like that toasted?" the new guy asked.

"No thank you," I replied as he handed me the tub of cream cheese and the bagel.

"I heard the cream cheese is to die for," he said as he handed me my cappuccino.

"I'll keep that in mind," I said with a smile.

I walked over to my usual table in the crowded café where Charlie and Dustin were already waiting.

"I hate coming here," Jenny complained as I sat down.

"Then don't," Dustin said curtly.

"I wish I could eat that bagel." She looked longingly at my bagel.

"I would share, but then again . . . ." I smiled as I spread the strawberry cream cheese over its surface.

"That's a good one." Dustin gave me a fist bump, which he used to try to steal some of my cream cheese.

I slapped his hand away. "Keep your dirty paws off my food!" I scowled and made sure to take every bit of cream cheese and spread it on my bagel.

"They're fingers, and you should learn how to share, with the living at least," Dustin replied, turning his smile into a pout just to prove to me how hungry he was.

"Buy your own food if you're so hungry!"

"I would, but I don't have an allowance to waste. I'm rather lacking in the job department." Dustin gave up on the pout and replaced it with his usual easy-going grin.

I licked my bagel all over just to prevent him from trying to steal it in the future.

"Aww, come on! You just destroyed a perfectly good bagel!" Jenny cried as I set it back down on the table.

"Why do you care? Food would just go straight through you," I told her. "Just like math class. Nothing would stick." I picked up my bagel once again.

"Alright, you've had your fun at my girlfriend," Charlie said, trying to be serious. "Cut it out."

"Whatever you say." I bit into my bagel and munched on it as obnoxiously as I could. But something seemed different with the bagel; it tasted funny. But I quickly forgot as Jenny continued to complain.

"I can't believe I'm saying this, but Dustin is better behaved than you are." Jenny scowled at me.

Dustin raised his nose and forced a serious look. "She's right, that's just low, Mimi."

I punched his arm and he laughed. "Says you! Weren't you the one who threw a cup of apple cider through her yesterday?"

"How was I supposed to know ghosts can't catch?"

Charlie let out a bark of laughter, which earned him an unseen glare from Jenny.

"It seems like someone missed the memo on how ghosts are made of energy, not matter," I replied, taking another bite out of my bagel.

"That doesn't stop her from short-circuiting the electrical box in my house every day," Charlie said once he regained control over his laughter.

"I don't do it on purpose!" she cried incredulously.

"She says that she's trying to destroy your electric bill," Dustin threw in.

"I did not! Mimi, you tell him!"

"She says it's not on purpose."

"Of course, you don't. You just enjoy it when I have to go out and fix it because my parents blame me." Charlie leaned back in his chair.

I smiled; it was just like old times. Nothing could have made those few sparkling moments any better.

But then it ended.

I finished off my bagel and looked around. "Oh crap!"

"Mimi, what is it?" Charlie asked.

"Teddy and Trisha, they just walked in," I replied.

"Don't tell me you're actually freaking out?" Dustin turned to look.

"No, I just don't want to get into another fight. My parents won't be so lenient this time," I replied, ducking under the table. Just the thought of being in actual trouble with my parents made my stomach roll.

"You are such a girl," Dustin told me, slipping the keys to his car, which he had parked out back, from his sweatshirt pocket to me under the table. He always locked it, even though nobody in this town would take it. Some habits die hard, I guess.

I took the keys, thankful that Dustin was allowing me to leave without making a huge scene and crawled out from under the table. All the dread of having to deal with Teddy was making me feel nauseated.

"You aren't actually leaving yet, are you Mimi?" Charlie asked, not wanting to be left with Dustin, but not wanting to go to school more.

"Yes, I am," I replied, beginning to head towards the door that led to the back alley, "I'll be waiting out in the car."

"And we'll be waiting here when you've come back to your senses." Jenny waved as I opened the door and slipped out into the alley.

That's when it really hit me; the nausea and lightheadedness. It hadn't been from the anxiety of renewing the fight, it came from something else entirely. I caught my balance against the wall, my black hair falling into my face.

"I told you that cream cheese was to die for." A voice came from before me, making my blood run cold.

I lifted my head and saw the guy who'd sold me the bagel. "You?" My head was spinning.

"What a coincidence that the day you get a funny tasting bagel, your ex comes in and you walk out into the alley. They'll say it's an overdose, that the sight of him with another girl pushed you over the edge. They won't know the truth." He took a step towards me and the light flickered on in my mind.

"You're the demon!" I managed, falling to my knees; it was getting hard to breathe. What was wrong with me?

He smiled, but his face was a blur, and the same with his features. I couldn't distinguish anything; not hair, not facial hair, not eyes, not cheekbones, not any other type of feature that separates us from each other, that makes us unique. Thinking back on it, I had the same problem in the café. Maybe it was demonic power, or maybe it was something else more plausible.

Like I'd been poisoned.

It must have shown in my eyes, because the demon began to laugh at that moment.

"I gave you a hint, Mortuus Loquis, I warned you to stay out of my way."

"So you poisoned me to get across your point?" That made no sense at all. "I don't even know how I'm in your way!"

The demon circled me. "Poor, poor Matilda Blake. So oblivious to what's right before her eyes," it taunted.

Terror grasped my heart. The demon knew my name, it knew my name. How could it know my name? I never told anyone it, never spoke it aloud, not if I could help it; names were too powerful, especially when you are dealing with the dead. Your name is what defines you, it's not just how you're identified; it's your identity. If that demon had my full name, then it had power over me; it could make me do horrible things, and I would be helpless.

But it didn't have my full name, it didn't even pronounce it right. It was taking a wild guess. I swallowed my fear, and replied, "Wow, you're awful at name guessing, not even close."

The demon hissed.

Right on! I just caught it in a bluff. Thank God I can keep a cool head, even when I'm dying. I smiled grimly to myself; what a great last feat, being able to outwit a demon with my dying breath. That might as well be written as the epithet on my gravestone: Here lies Matilda Blake, a woman so cunning she outwitted a demon with her dying breath. Hopefully, they'd make it sound cooler than that.

The demon quit pacing around me, certain that I was dying, and conjured a locket out of thin air. The designs on it matched the exact designs I'd seen only a few times before. It was just like the locket Dustin gave me.

I gasped. "Where'd you get that?" I demanded.

"This?" It smiled, as if taking notice to the locket for the first time. "You know what it can do. Good, that means you know what I plan to do." It lazily twisted the locket around in its hands, now in complete control.

"You killed Jenny," I accused, taking a stab at bluffing, "and that's why you're killing me, because it's her soul you want, not mine." The realization hit me square in the face.

The demon laughed, sending a shiver down my spine. "Is that what you believe, little child?" it mocked. "I feel so cheated, I was hoping you'd figure it out before you lost your soul. Yes, I did kill your little friend, and yes, you did prevent me from taking her soul, but it was never her soul I truly wanted. No, her soul, and the others, have only been to pass the time. Child's play, really. No, you do not have the answer, nor will you ever have it."

"Why are you doing this?" I demanded. I sounded like a child whose parents wouldn't allow them to have their Xbox back because they were failing school. I didn't understand, and it was completely unfair.

"Ah, if I told you, then you would be at peace. No, I want your soul to be in agony when I take it. A tormented soul is far better."

I could feel my life slipping away from me. My body was burning, my entire existence turned into complete agony. The pain was so great I almost began writhing on the ground; the pain worked itself into my mind as well. But I couldn't go down, not like this. The demon wasn't going to get my soul. "It won't work, you'll never get what you want!"

"We'll see about that." It chuckled and disappeared, leaving me to die alone.

I'm dying. The words crossed my mind before I could stop them. I was going to die, alone, in an alley, with people mere yards away. I didn't want to die. I had so much to live for! There were so many things I hadn't done, so many things I had to say!

My arms were becoming too weak to hold myself up from the ground. I was going to die in this alley, all alone. Everyone was going to think I committed suicide, even Charlie, Jenny, and Dustin. I couldn't go on existing if I did that to them, I didn't deserve anything but an eternity rotting in hell if that happened. I laughed coldly to myself; that's exactly what's going to happen. That demon wasn't going to let my soul go to heaven, not after what it told me it was going to do. Besides, another soul for it to add to its collection, no way it was going to pass up that opportunity.

I wanted to weep, to wallow in my tears, but I couldn't. I had to survive. No way in hell was I going to give up that easily. Matilda Blake does not go down without a fight, not now, not ever. Trisha's broken nose was proof of that!

There had to be some strength left, something that hadn't been used to fight the poison. I heaved myself towards the door, trying my hardest not to fail. I just about reached it, pulling myself across the grime-covered asphalt, when my strength went out. My arms collapsed under me, giving me a face-full of asphalt.

This was it. I was officially a goner. It was the end of the line for me.

The door to the alley opened and out walked Teddy. He looked down and saw me, dying on the pavement, and had the sense to cry, "AMBULANCE! CALL AN AMBULANCE!" He then dropped to my side. "Stay with me, M!" he said, turning me onto my back. His face was livid, his cheekbones were more pronounced, adding to his ratty face. His blue eyes were wide with horror, he didn't know what to do. Vivid features, that kicked out the possibility that the poison was screwing with my perception skills.

Dustin came running out next. "MIMI!" he cried in alarm, jumping to my side as well. "Oh God! How'd this happen?" He knelt next to me and lifted my head up, lowering his so he could hear if I was still breathing.

"Demon . . . poison," I breathed into his ear.

His face went pale. Strangely, I couldn't help but think that his reaction was more because he didn't have an antidote to demon poison in his pockets.

"Give me a hand!" Dustin commanded Teddy. "Keep her head level. If she stops breathing, give her CPR. If her heart stops beating, you start pounding on her chest to the tune of 'I've been working on the railroad,' you got it?" He pulled out his Swiss army knife and a tube, along with a few IV needles.

"What do you think you're trying to do?" Teddy demanded as he slipped his fingers under my head to cradle it.

"I'm trying to save her life," Dustin replied, slipping one of the IV needles into my arm, and attaching the tube to it. "She needs new blood; her blood's been poisoned."

"Poisoned?" Teddy repeated in shock. "How do you know?"

"She told me, and she has clear signs of it too." Dustin rolled up his sleeve.

Teddy grabbed his hand, somehow managing to hold my head in the other without moving it. "Her blood type is B negative. You'll kill her if you give her your blood."

"And how do you know that?" Dustin demanded.

"We did a lab in science once. If you give her any other blood type, she'll die."

"If I don't give her blood, she's going to die!" Dustin snarled.

"Not mine, I have B negative too," Teddy replied, rolling up his sleeve.

Dustin nodded his head, then put the other needle into Teddy's vein. The scarlet fluid began to flow down the tube just as I passed out.

From there, I remember only glimpses.

I saw flashing red and blue lights; I heard sirens wailing, people shouting. Everything was a blur. I remember seeing Dustin's face, calling out his name, but he wouldn't come. Why wouldn't he come?

Then there were doctors wearing blue scrubs, bright lights, and an annoying beeping sound. Lastly, there was pain, unspeakable pain. I knew I was screaming even though I couldn't hear it. I just wanted it to stop, for it all to be over.

And then it was.

* * *

I opened my eyes to a bright room. It hurt to see all that light, so I scrunched my eyes, blinking profusely to adjust them.

I'm dead.

The thought crossed my mind and in an instant, my heart rate skyrocketed. I tried to move but I couldn't, something was holding me in place, tugging on my arms. Hyperv-entilating, I clawed at my arms, trying to release them when something grabbed me.

It was Dustin.

"Dustin! I'm so sorry! I didn't want to die; I didn't want to go! The bagel, it was poisoned and then I collapsed in the alley and I didn't want to die! I wanted to live! Please forgive me!" I wept, saying everything slightly slurred and almost too fast to understand. I'm still surprised Dustin got the gist of what I was saying.

"Mimi, you're not dead!" He sounded overjoyed.

I stopped moving. "I'm not . . . dead?" That beeping noise was going crazy again and I wanted to break it. "Make the beeping stop!" I began swiping at the air and Dustin had to grab my arms to contain me.

"Mimi, you need to relax, or the nurses are going to kick me out," he said gently, his golden eyes staring directly into mine, calming me down.

"Nurses?" I asked, still confused.

"Yes, you're in a hospital. You got lucky; another minute and you would have been a goner." He leaned down and kissed my forehead.

"In the alley, you saved my life." My thoughts were still fuzzy, but that much was clear.

"No, I didn't," he said.

"But you did! I saw you; you did a blood transfusion and saved my life. You're my hero," I insisted. Why did he deny it?

"Mimi, you're drugged right now. You were screaming so loudly that the only way to stop the pain was to put you on morphine. You're highly delusional."

"And you're lying." I began to laugh but it hurt.

"Is everything alright in there?" A nurse came rushing in. She took one look at me and gasped. "She's awake!"

"Yeah, I'm awake. Whoa, what does that button do?" I reached out to press the red button, but Dustin set it out of my reach.

"We don't need the entire nursing staff running in here, Mimi," he said with a laugh.

The nurse laughed as well. "I'll say it's a miracle for sure. We all thought you were going to die, Miss Matilda, you were in a coma for three days."

"Coma, like what the butterflies go through?" My brain was out of it, that's how many drugs they had me on.

"That's a cocoon, dear," Dustin explained.

"Oh, those too." I smiled at him.

"How long is she going to be like this?" Dustin asked, trying not to sound so enthusiastic.

"At least six more hours, she had her last dose half an hour ago," the nurse replied.

"Good, this is going to be fun." Dustin smiled deviously.

The door opened and Mom and Dad came walking into the room. "Matilda, you're awake!" Mom exclaimed, rushing to me. She went straight through the nurse we were just talking to.

"Mom," I said, staring at her with my eyes wide, "you just walked through the nurse."

"What are you talking about, Mimi? The nurses are all outside."

"It's the morphine talking, Mrs. Blake. They gave her the last dose half an hour ago." Dustin told her. It wasn't the complete truth, but enough to convince my mom.

"No, you still walked through the nurse," I insisted as my mother gave me a hug. "Ask Dustin, we were just talking to her."

"It's alright, Miss Matilda, your folks can't see me, I'm a ghost," the nurse explained.

"Mimi, is it possible you're seeing the ghost of an image you saw earlier?" Dad asked.

Dustin raised his eyebrows. "Don't tell me you didn't say 'hi' to the nurse?"

"Nurse or no nurse, I'm just glad our baby is okay." Mom hugged me again and I sneezed in her hair.

They got a lot of good blackmail the next couple days after I became conscious. When they tell you in school about how drugs such as cocaine are bad, listen, because I've been on morphine and I don't even remember half the stuff I did. That's why I'm skipping ahead a few days.

Dustin only left my side after visiting hours were over. As it turns out, I missed the last days of school due to my being in a coma (so much for those detentions), and Dustin didn't have a summertime job, unlike my parents and Charlie. I didn't really have any visitors during my stay in the hospital other than Charlie and Dustin because I wasn't exactly well-known by the rest of the student body. I preferred it that way though.

It was my last night in the hospital that they finally took me off all the drugs. They wanted to see if I was going to manage after the hell I went through, you know, with the almost dying and everything. My parents had gone down to eat in the hospital cafeteria, leaving me alone with Dustin.

"So, you're going home in the morning?" Dustin asked randomly.

"Yeah, if I can manage the night, which won't be a problem," I replied with a smile. Truthfully, I was ready to get out of there from day one. I hate hospitals. People think that graveyards are full of death, but hospitals are full of diseases and people who are dying, and I find that horrifying. Also, I was tired of being harassed by every ghost that walked the halls. The second they find out that someone can see them, they flock like sheep, begging you to help them, listen to them, and even pass on messages to their loved ones. I think I managed to help sixty ghosts during the week-long stay. Dustin managed about forty-two.

"That's almost too bad; I enjoy our days in the hospital." He winked to show that he was only slightly serious.

"Pity," I replied, and he laughed.

"It's nice to have you sane again; your confusion was beginning to bore me," he said, sitting down on the edge of my bed.

"Liar, Liar! You took advantage of my fragile brain and videotaped it!" I kicked him and he slid back off the bed.

"You know," he began, walking towards the front of my bed, "we should talk about what happened." He stopped and sat down in the chair on the right-hand side.

"Now?" I asked.

He was about to reply, but there was a knock at the door. Two men walked in and I recognized them as Detectives Roland and Myers; they worked at the station. "Sorry to trouble you, Miss Blake. I'm Detective Roland, and this is my partner, Detective Myers. We're here to ask you a few questions," said the detective wearing the nice blue jeans and light leather jacket.

"I'll just step out for a moment," Dustin said, getting to his feet, but I grabbed his arm.

"Stay," I said.

He sat back down.

The two Detectives pulled up two chairs and sat down on the left side of the bed. Detective Myers pulled a scratchpad from the inside pocket of his blazer and uncapped his pen.

"This will only take a minute," Detective Myers said.

I nodded. "Ask away."

Myers nodded. "Would you tell us why you ended up in the alley behind the café?"

"I went back there because I was heading out to Dustin's car. He parked in the parking lot at the other end of the alley," I replied.

"Alone?"

"Yes, you see, my ex-boyfriend and his new girlfriend had just walked in."

"And why did that make you leave?"

"Because a few days before, his new girlfriend and I got into a fight. I didn't want to renew it, so I went to wait outside until they left."

Truth.

Myers scribbled notes onto his notepad and nodded.

"Do you know what poisoned you, Miss Blake?" asked Detective Roland.

"Yes, the strawberry cream cheese."

Also true.

"And how do you know that?" asked Myers.

Okay, so maybe my brain still wasn't intact as well as it needed to be.

I closed my eyes; my throat was constricting as my brain accessed the memory for the first time. I felt a hand on my arm, and I opened my eyes.

It was Dustin's. "It's okay, tell them, Mimi."

I nodded and took a deep breath. "When I had bought my food, the new employee there had remarked upon how the strawberry cream cheese was to die for. I saw him again in the alley as I began to blackout. He told me he had poisoned it, but he didn't tell me why." My voice was trembling. I hadn't realized just how scared I was.

"Do you remember what this man looked like?" Roland questioned.

I shook my head. "I can't remember much of anything." Tears were streaming from my eyes now. I wished they would stop but they wouldn't. I was back in that alley, reliving the horror of being poisoned and slowly dying alone on the cold pavement.

"Are those all your questions?" Dustin stood up; I could hear the anger in his voice. He was outraged that they would make me cry; outraged they would assume anything other than an attempt on my life.

"Only a few more," Detective Myers replied calmingly.

Dustin didn't sit back down.

"Dustin, it's okay, I want them to get this lunatic," I said softly.

He looked at me and his face softened. Slowly, he sank back down to his seat.

"Do you have any enemies, Miss Blake?"

"She's seventeen; of course she doesn't have any enemies!" Dustin burst out.

"Dustin, relax. They're doing their jobs," I quieted him. "But no, I don't think I have any enemies."

"Then that makes this a serial killer." Detective Roland stood up.

"A what?!" I squeaked. I felt my heart-rate jump.

"You mean there have been more killings?" Dustin was just as surprised as I was.

"Yes, but his victims have been random. He targets young adults and teens, but there's no links and the victims have all died, except you. You were very lucky, Miss Blake, but we suspect he'll come back to finish the job," Roland explained, replacing his notepad in his blazer.

"We can offer you police protection." Myers added.

I again shook my head. "No, I don't want it."

"But he may come after you again," Myers stressed.

"I don't care; I want to be a kid. I don't want to be reminded for the next—however long—that I'm a victim of a serial killer. I appreciate your offer, but I refuse either way."

"Alright then. Goodnight, Miss Blake," Detective Roland said.

"We may need to ask you more questions in the future." Detective Myers also stood up.

"Whatever I can do to help." I smiled weakly.

The two men nodded then left.

Emotionally exhausted, I laid my head back on the pillow and closed my eyes; the dam holding back my emotions broke, and I laid helpless in its wake.

Dustin moved his hand into mine and squeezed it tightly. "Mimi, I'm right here," he said soothingly. "I won't let anything get you."

"It's not me it wants."

"What?"

I took a shattered breath and elaborated. "The demon told me that it's after something else, along with Jenny, and it was killing people for sport, a way to pass the time, until it got what it wanted. It tried to kill me because I was getting in the way. It probably stole Jenny's soul; I haven't seen her since I went out into the alley to die." I sobbed. I didn't care that I was crying in front of Dustin, I was glad he was there.

"Hey, it's alright." Dustin got off the chair and sat next to me on the bed. "In the commotion you caused, I forced Jenny back into the locket, fearing . . . ."

"You thought I would crossover with her." My voice caught in my throat.

Dustin looked away in shame. "I was scared and selfish. I saw your essence begin to rise out of your body, Mimi; I thought I'd lost you."

I hugged him and cried on his shoulder. "I thought I'd lost you too!"

He wrapped his arms around me and held me tightly. "Don't do that ever again." His voice was strained as he held back tears of his own.

I cried harder. We sat there, just holding each other until I finally could grab a hold of myself again. I sniffed and wiped my face with my arms and the palms of my hands.

"Are you going to be okay?" Dustin asked.

I nodded. "Yeah, thank you."

He smiled and stood up. "Visiting hours are almost up," he said sadly, looking at the clock.

"You're not going to leave yet, are you?" I sounded desperate even in my own ears.

He raised his brows. "No, not yet."

"Good." I let go of my breath and closed my eyes. I hadn't realized I had fallen asleep until I awoke the next morning to find him gone.

CHAPTER SEVEN:

"So, you finally found out," Jenny said. She looked ashamed, not making eye contact with me.

"Yes. Why didn't you tell me?"

"Because I didn't want you to get hurt and go on a warpath!" Jenny burst. She threw her hands over her mouth. "I'm sorry, Mimi, this is all my fault."

I stood up and looked out my open bedroom window. It was the first night back in my room; everything was still how I had left it the morning I got poisoned, so coming back was overwhelming.

For some reason, when something life changing happens to you, you expect the whole world to change overnight. It doesn't. Just because you change, doesn't mean anything else has.

"Is that why you didn't crossover? Because you were afraid that I would find out the truth and hunt down the demon?"

"No, I was afraid it'd come after you." Her voice was soft with tears.

I turned to face her. "Why, did it tell you it would?"

She shook her head and wiped her ghost tears with the sleeve of her shirt. "I don't know. I never really thought about it but this demon—when I was dying, it told me something that I think you should hear."

"What did it tell you, Jenny?" I walked over and sat down. Just standing for a few minutes was exhausting in my weakened state.

Jenny took an unnecessary deep breath, then she started saying something, but changed to say: "It told me about this kid it hanged. First, it made him write a suicide note, giving fake reasons for killing himself so that his Mortuus Loquis friend wouldn't ask questions. Next, it forced him to hang the rope by which he would hang from the rafters and then—" Jenny burst into tears, "—it made him jump and he asphyxiated! The demon stole his soul, Mimi; it took his soul! When I sat there dying, I knew it would do the same to mine, which is why I called you. I didn't want to leave you thinking I killed myself. I couldn't do that to you!"

I stood up and tried to give her a hug, forgetting that I would just pass through her. Electricity zinged through my body like a shot of energy. "Jenny, you never had to worry about that. You should have just told me from the beginning and then I would have protected you better. I would have damned that demon back to where it came from."

Jenny didn't say anything, but I could see the burden had finally lifted from her shoulders.

I was about to say more but there was a knock on my door.

"Mimi, may I come in?" It was my father.

"Sure Dad, come in," I replied.

The door opened and he walked in. He was wearing his suit, apparently about to head out to a wake. In two long strides, he was at the foot of my bed and sat down. "Mimi, there's something we need to talk about."

"This looks confidential, I'll come back later," Jenny said, and began to glide towards the door.

"This involves you, Jennifer, so you'd better stay," Dad said quickly.

I swung my head around to look at him. "You can see her?"

"Yes," was his simple reply, "and that's what I am here to talk to you about." He gestured for me to take a seat on the bed.

I sat down next to him and Jenny floated closer. "Why didn't you tell me you could see ghosts?"

"Because I figured you knew," he replied with a smile. "Most Mortuus Loquis recognize each other at first glance; it's all in the eyes."

I looked at him curiously. "What do you mean by that?"

"Your eyes are gold, Mimi, who else do you know has gold eyes?"

I thought about it for a moment. In truth, I knew only two other people with gold eyes, Dad and Dustin. "What you're saying is that if I meet someone with gold eyes, they're a Mortuus Loquis?"

"That or they're a vampire wannabe," Jenny mumbled.

"Dad, how come you can see ghosts, but none of my uncles or aunts on your side of the family can?" I asked, not quite understanding.

Dad sighed and looked around the room. "From what I understand, it's completely unpredictable how many children will carry the gift. I was two of six, but your grandmother and her brothers all could see as well. We come from a long line of Mortuus Loquis, dating all the way back to England during the eighteenth century."

"England in the eighteenth century?" Jenny whistled. "Your family is old."

"Everyone's family is old. It's a matter of knowing where you came from that's the difference." I shushed her.

"I came from Spain."

"That's great Jenny."

"I know. Hang on, wasn't William Blake an Englishman of the eighteenth century?" Jenny asked.

"Yes, we are descendants of his family, he never had children of his own," Dad explained.

I stared at Jenny.

"What? I pay attention in English every so often," Jenny said with dignity.

"So, we're related to William Blake?"

"In the flesh," Dad said with a nod.

The puzzle clicked together. "Isn't it said that he saw his brother's soul rise from his body after his brother died?"

"Very good, Mimi, you know a little about our family history." Dad smiled. "Yes, he was open about his gift, and everyone thought he was crazy."

"But isn't that why we have this gift, to share it with others?"

"Death is a sensitive subject to everyone, Mimi, and I want you to remember this: no matter how comfortable you feel about it, it's a misdirection. Remember that." He stood up and headed for the door. "Oh, and Jenny, quit blowing the circuitry, I'm tired of fixing it." He closed the door behind him.

"Wow, I think that was the shortest conversation I've ever seen your dad have." Jenny whistled, which is an accomplishment, considering she doesn't actually breathe.

"I think you're right." I was a little shocked myself.

"Do you think he's sick or something? Maybe I should go check on him." She began to float towards the wall.

"Or you could stay, I hate being left alone." I was tired of being clever; I just wanted someone to keep me company.

"Poor baby, it must kill you to be so truthful." Jenny gave me a mock smile.

"Fine, get the hell out of my room."

Jenny laughed. "I'll be back in a few minutes." Then she floated through the wall.

"Man, I never thought she would leave." A voice came from my window.

I jumped and spun around. It was Dustin. "Holy cow! You gave me a heart attack!"

"Sorry about that," he said as he crawled through the open window, "but I was just trying to be sneaky. Your mom sent me home because she didn't want you overexcited tonight."

I walked over to his side as he stood up. "So, you decided my window was the next best 'unexciting' option?" I gave him an amused smile.

"It was that or the stairs. I thought the window would be a little more discrete."

"How long were you out there for?"

"Only half an hour."

I cast my eyes towards the floor. "You heard my conversation with Jenny."

He lifted my chin softly with his finger. "Don't be ashamed. I did hear the conversation, but I wasn't about to go broaching the subject unless you wanted me to."

I nodded my head and felt the dizziness kick in. I began to swoon, but Dustin caught me and helped me to my bed.

"Are you sure you should be home?" he asked.

"Dustin, I'm fine. I'm just a little lightheaded yet."

"I don't buy it, Mimi, not one word. Maybe I should go."

"No!" I grabbed his arm then quickly released it.

Dustin paused in mid-action, confused.

"I mean, please stay." I felt the blush deepen on my cheeks.

He looked at me, and I could see the battle going on inside his head: if he stayed, that would be trouble, but if he left, that would be trouble. If he didn't make a quick decision, that would also be trouble.

I decided to make the decision for him. "Dustin, I need answers from you, and you need answers from me. Don't you remember what you told me that day in the park? We need each other, Dustin. And I'm beginning to realize just how much I need you."

"But not tonight." Dustin walked over to the window. "Mimi, forget everything I've told you. Forget what happened yesterday—hell, forget the past two months. I'm no good for you, Meems."

I ran over to the window and grabbed his arm. "Dustin, please!" I begged him.

He looked me in the eyes, and I saw how much it hurt him to tell me all of this. "Mimi, you're weak, and you're suffering from a case of heroic love. I am not your hero, Teddy is. He was the one to find you in the alley, not me, so if you're going to fall for anyone, choose him."

"Dustin Harold Harper! Would you just listen to me for one second?" My temper flared and I was on the verge of screaming at him. My words became more powerful as I invoked his name, causing him to freeze in mid-action. He couldn't leave if he wanted to. "Do you not understand that it wasn't Teddy who saved my life? It was you! You're the one who had the knowledge to save my life before the medics arrived. If it weren't for you, I'd be on a metal slab at the county morgue, another casualty due to our demonic friend. It was you who I saw in my dreams, your name that I cried out for. You were the one there for me, not Teddy, not anybody else. I don't know what your deal is with this sudden disinterest, but I know that you feel the same way I do. Don't leave me hanging."

He leaned down and kissed my forehead. "I'm sorry," he apologized. "I will be back tomorrow, I promise."

I held tightly onto his arm. "Dustin."

He gently put his palm up to my cheek. "Mimi, I'm sorry for what I said, but I still mean it. I'm not good for you."

"Maybe I don't want good, ever think of that?"

"But you deserve good."

"Then don't sell yourself short."

Our eyes locked. My knees were trembling, but I wasn't about to back down. I stood my ground, trying to be as strong as I needed to be.

He sighed and took a step away from the window. "You drive a hard bargain."

"So I've been told," I replied, beginning to feel dizzy.

Dustin bent down and lifted me into his arms. "Stubborn. That's what you are; a stubborn pain in the butt."

"I am not stubborn, and I'm definitely not an a-hole," I said in a weak voice. I could feel the earth spinning around me, making me feel lightheaded and sick.

Dustin lightly placed me on my bed and then sat down next to me. "You really like having me around," he said with a smile.

I nuzzled my head on his chest. "Yes, I do."

"Does Jenny?"

I looked up into his eyes. "Why do you ask?"

His silence made me remember what Jenny said the demon had told her about. That kid that hung himself.

"Oh my God, Dustin, it was talking about you, you're the Mortuus Loquis! That was your friend." Guilt suddenly overwhelmed me; Dustin had kept it to himself, that's why he'd been acting weird since he walked in. He knew that this wasn't the first place that the demon had attacked. "I'm sorry, I should have known."

"No, I'm the one who should be sorry," he said, his voice hardly audible. "I knew that something was screwy with his suicide, but I was so upset that I didn't even think that some otherworldly being had something to do with it."

"You can't blame yourself for that demon killing him, Dustin," I said, trying to reason with him.

"How can't I? If I'd have—"

"Been inhuman and not mourned for your friend? I didn't even know that a demon killed my friend, and she's been harassing me for the past three months about it."

"That demon was in Chicago with me. There were a bunch of suicides, starting with my parents and ending with my best friend. Mimi, that demon is haunting me, trying to make me commit suicide."

"Dustin, there's gotta be something else going on. Why would a demon just come after you, a single Mortuus Loquis? You're not the reason for the demon."

He looked towards the window. "You don't know that, Mimi. Just last week you were on your deathbed."

"Hey," I grabbed his hand, "I'm here now, aren't I? What happened wasn't your fault; it wasn't anybody's fault but the demon."

"I wish I could believe you, but you don't even believe that." Dustin turned to face me. "Mimi, people who get close to me have the tendency to get killed. My parents and my best friend are already pushing up daisies! I wouldn't be able to live with myself if anything were to happen to you because I got too close; I'm already putting you in harm's way."

"How do you know that I'm not the one putting you in harm's way?" I countered quickly. "Think about it, the demon threatened me for getting in the way. You can't take the credit!"

"Mimi, take a step into my shoes. What would you do if tomorrow the demon came after me and stole my soul?! Would you be able to live with yourself, with the knowledge that you could have prevented my fate?"

"Dustin, I would do everything in my power to prevent that from happening, and if it did happen, I wouldn't be able to blame myself."

Dustin let out a laugh. "You're something else, Mimi." He leaned over and our faces were inches apart. "I wish I could kiss you," he said softly, touching my hand.

"You could. I won't stop you."

He retreated ever so slightly. "That's what I'm afraid of."

I leaned back and put my head on my pillow. "So that's it then? We're just going to keep ignoring everything and hang in this limbo forever?"

Dustin stood up. "I'll stop by tomorrow, Mimi."

"Don't bother; I'm going to Charlie's," I said quietly.

He didn't say anything, but I knew he was hurt. He deserved it. I listened as he climbed out the window, somehow managing to close it after him.

The lights flickered a bit, and then I saw Jenny float through the wall out of the corner of my eye.

"Is it safe to assume you heard a majority of what we said?" I asked her grumpily.

"Yes," Jenny replied cautiously.

I sighed and put a pillow over my face, screaming into the picture of Spider-Man. Why did he have to leave me? Why did he have to go?

I felt energy near my shoulder, and I removed the pillow, revealing my swollen pink eyes and raw runny nose. "Jenny, I don't want to do this anymore."

She leaned her translucent head on my shoulder. "I know, I know. He's a boy; they're insanely bipolar and uncertain. He'll come crawling back to you in the morning, I know he will."

"But what if he doesn't?" I asked her. "Then what am I supposed to do?!"

Jenny floated up, "Then you go after him. Matilda, he's the best guy that's ever happened to you, no matter what our differences are, he's the guy for you! And this dance that the two of you have created, it's just a way of postponing reality. I want you to be happy, Mimi, and he is what makes you happy."

I wanted to hug her; this was the first time I'd ever heard her say something supportive. I was about to reply when I heard a faint knocking sound on the door.

Someone was there.

With stealth, I crossed the room and quickly pulled it open, peering out into the hall. There was no one in sight. I shrugged, maybe I imagined it.

I closed the door and returned to my bed. I was so exhausted from all the drama in the last few minutes that my head was spinning. I dropped down onto my pillow and was asleep before I even had the chance to register that I had.

It's just too bad that it was the last night I'd be spending at home for a long time.

CHAPTER EIGHT:

I woke up to an energy surge in my stomach.

Jenny had found the need to stick her hand through my stomach until I jolted to a sitting position, wide awake.

"What the hell do you think you're doing?" I demanded angrily. I had been sleeping so peacefully; it was the first night that I didn't have one of those weird hospital dreams. It felt nice not seeing the Muppets as I slept for once.

"It's your mom; she called the people at the blue house. She's having you admitted!" Jenny said; a terrified expression glued to her face.

I felt a cold hand clutch my heart; the blue house is what we call the asylum in town. My worst nightmare was coming true; I was going to be locked in the crazy bin with a bunch of psychopaths for the rest of my life.

"Jenny, how long do I have to get out?" I asked, trying to keep my calm.

"Not long, maybe five minutes max. But she's got the door covered, how do you plan on getting out?"

I looked at the window. "The same way I always do when I need to escape," I replied, sliding out of bed and carefully walking to my closet. I was still wearing the same clothes from last night, but I didn't have time to change. Opening my closet, I grabbed the emergency pack I had hanging on the inside hook and threw it over my shoulder. This thing was packed for survival; I could survive a week at least.

"Mimi, there's no way in hell you can climb out your window in the shape you're in!" Jenny said in protest. "You should just go and then show them you're sane. It'll take only a few days."

I shook my head. "Do you wanna know what will happen? They'll strap me to a machine and ask me questions like, 'Do you believe you can see ghosts?' or 'How long have you been having these hallucinations?' and if I lie and say I can't, they'll know. I'll be locked up there forever while they do experiments on me with medications that will make me just as psychotic as the rest of the people there. They'll probably think I'm schizophrenic or something. Jenny, I have to run."

"You watch way too many movies," Jenny said, shaking her head. "But I see your point, yet, the window is still a bad idea."

The doorbell rang downstairs, signaling that the loony bin people were here to cart me away for life. It was now or never.

I opened the window.

A soft breeze floated through, filling the room with the warm summer air. Suddenly, an idea popped into my mind. I quickly walked to my desk and moved the chair so that it was under the knob, making it near impossible to open the door. They were going to have a hell of a time catching me. I returned to the window. "Jenny, I can't be distracted by you, so I need you to do something for me."

"Sure, anything."

I took the locket out of my pocket; the one Dustin had trapped her in while I was in the hospital. "I need you to come back inside here."

"No way!" she protested.

"You said anything," I insisted.

"Well I take it back, anything except for that! I will not be manhandled like some kind of doll, Matilda! I won't do it!"

"Jenny, if I were to lose track of you, for even a moment, then I could get caught. I need to be sure where you are, just for right now, and I'll let you out as soon as I'm safe enough to talk to you," I promised, opening the locket.

Jenny gave the locket a look of disdain. "Alright, fine, just for you, but I will come back and haunt you if you don't keep that promise."

I smiled at her. "Thank you."

"Yeah, yeah, sure." She reached out and touched the locket, then disappeared as it snapped shut, locking her inside.

I threw it around my neck and tucked it under my shirt, feeling the cool metal against my chest. It was time to go. I was about to climb out when there was a soft tapping at my door.

"Mimi, are you awake?" Mom's voice asked through the door.

"Ah, yeah, just putting on some clothes," I lied, preparing to jump to the tree.

"Alright, we have company so come down when you're ready."

Like that was going to happen. "Okay," I said then took the leap.

I managed to hook my arms around the branch of the maple. If my breathing was heavy just from managing this, how was I supposed to escape? Taking a deep breath, I climbed down the tree and took off into the garden, leaping over the gate and through the neighbor's yard.

Something in the back of my mind told me to jump into the bushes. I'm not sure what it was, but I listened and was lucky enough to just miss a couple of white gowned people pass by a foot from my hiding spot. My heart started beating over-time; Mom had planned for my windowed escape. Another couple of seconds and my life would have been at the mercy of a bunch of money grubbing, fake-helping, so-called doctors.

When they were over the gate, I darted out into the street and speed-dialed Charlie. I made at a practical pace towards the river, the only place I figured I could lose any pursuit, no matter what they were using. No longer was I a normal kid, I was a fugitive. The pool of people I could trust dwindled down to two: Charlie and Dustin.

Charlie answered on the second ring. "Hello?"

"Charlie, I need some help."

"Well, turn around and say so. I can see you've got your pack," he replied.

I spun around and saw him walking down the street towards me, the sun bouncing off his glasses.

"Charlie!" I felt relief flow through my veins.

"Mimi, what are you doing?" he asked, a puzzled smile on his face.

"I'm on the run, my mom called the crazy bin and is having me admitted."

The smile faded from his face. "You're kidding."

I shook my head. "Charlie, I don't know what to do, but I can't stop now, it's already too late and I've got to keep moving."

"Come with me, I've got my car, I could give you a lift anywhere you want to go," Charlie said, pulling me towards the beat-up Chevy on the side of the street.

"Wouldn't that make you an accessory?" I asked, worried about his involvement.

"The second I ran into you that happened, it's not like they could do anything though, I can always claim ignorance and give them a false location to search." He opened the side door for me.

I smiled. "Thanks Charlie," I said and climbed into the car.

He hopped into the driver's seat and switched on the engine. It started with an obnoxious *VROOOM* which made me flinch. This was the loudest get-a-way of all times.

Charlie began to drive away and I looked out the back window, half expecting to see a white clad doctor come running after us. Luckily, none did.

I sank down in my seat a little; I was good for now.

"So, Miss Teenager-on-the-run, where to?" Charlie asked.

"The river," I said instantly.

"Okay." He turned down the street and started working his way to the river. "Where do you plan to go after this?" he asked.

"Somewhere, I'm not exactly sure yet. I know there's a forest a couple miles downstream, so I'll probably try to reach it."

He began to slow down. "That isn't much of a plan."

"I don't have time to come up with a plan, Charlie! I'm making it up as I go. A little support would be nice," I shouted at him. Truthfully, I knew he was right, but I was freaking out and I didn't want him to remind me how doomed I was.

"Sorry, I'll try to keep my concern for your well-being out of it, then," he replied acidly.

We reached the river and he pulled to a complete stop.

"You could come back to my house; my parents love you; they'd keep you safe."

I shook my head. "I'm sorry for snapping, Charlie, I'm just scared. But I can't go back to your house, that's just putting too much blame on you, and my mom would press charges."

"It's alright, just don't get killed." Charlie waved it off.

I gave him a hug. "You're a life-saver," I told him, then climbed out of the Chevy.

He quickly drove off, knowing it was best not to be seen dropping me off in a secluded area of town.

I took a deep breath, then slowly climbed down the hill towards the river. Years ago, while on a family picnic, I invented this escape route. Even as a little girl, I was terrified of what my parents would do if they discovered my gift. Now, I find that all that fretting wasn't for nothing. A year ago, I had hidden a small kayak in the bushes down here, thinking that if I ever needed it, it would be ready to use.

Reaching the bottom of the hill, I eagerly began to search the bushes for my salvation.

All I found was a single paddle.

So much for that great idea.

"Mimi! Mimi!" I heard a voice calling out my name.

I was horrified; caught before I'd even gotten out of town.

"MIMI! WHAT ARE YOU DOING?"

I turned to find that Dustin was on a small fishing boat that was trolling down the river. He and some older gentleman were holding fishing rods. Dustin waved at me like a crazed lunatic, trying to grab my attention.

Relief, once again, flowed through me and I waved back. "HEY! CAN I HITCH A RIDE?" I called from across the water.

Dustin turned and had a short conversation with the gentleman, then jumped into the pilot's seat and drove the craft to me, beaching it on the bank. He hopped off the craft and smiled at me. "Aren't you a little weak to have traveled this far?" he asked.

I glanced at the guy still on the boat and my decision to call him over wavered. Maybe I should have dove into the bushes again.

Dustin saw my hesitation and laughed. "Oh, this is my uncle, the one I've been staying with since my parents died. Uncle Ted, this is my friend Matilda. Matilda, this is Uncle Ted."

Uncle Ted gave me an uninterested nod. He most likely wanted to continue with his fishing trip before all the crappies stopped biting.

I pulled Dustin over, hoping that we'd be out of earshot from his uncle.

"Dustin, my mom called the asylum. She wants to have me admitted," I whispered, fearing that Uncle Ted might hear.

The blood drained from Dustin's face. "I had an uncle who could see sent to one, he never got out. He committed suicide after three months because he couldn't tell the living from the dead. Those places are messed up, Mimi."

"I know that, why do you think I'm running?!" I whispered franticly.

Dustin glanced over at his uncle, who was playing with his casting reel. "Uncle Ted, we've got a major situation," Dustin said, causing Uncle Ted's head to rise and look at us for the first time.

I gasped; his eyes were golden too!

"Well, if it isn't another Mortuus Loquis!" Uncle Ted said with a grin. "Why didn't you tell me she was one of us before?"

Dustin rolled his eyes. "I thought it was obvious due to her eyes, Uncle."

I held back a smirk; I didn't want to make a bad impression with his uncle if that was my only way out.

"Well, Miss Matilda, is it? What can we help you with?" Uncle Ted asked, putting his line down and crossing to the closer side of the boat.

I bit my lip, I hated having to talk to strangers.

Fortunately, Dustin did the talking for me. "Uncle, her mom's trying to admit her to an institute; we have to help her run."

Uncle Ted nodded his head. "Hop in the boat, dear. They'll be coming here soon, since this was the first place you thought of."

"How'd you—?"

"Know? Simple: all people run to the first place they can think of. It's a survival instinct. It's running to the second place that catches them off-guard," Uncle Ted explained.

I climbed into the boat with Dustin's assistance. I was really tired from all the running and hiding and standing and was ready to pass out.

Dustin pushed the boat back out into the river and hopped aboard, sending water droplets all over the place. He looked determined, his jaw set in a tense line and his eyes dead-set on the river which lay before us.

A feeling of gratitude shot through me. I was lucky to have Dustin as my friend, luckier than anyone in the world. Dustin knew what he was doing, and he didn't care about the consequences of his actions, he only cared about one thing: helping others.

As it turns out, that's his fatal flaw too.

The boat turned into a small boat house about a mile down the river. I only knew this because I was staring skywards in the craft when there was suddenly a roof over my head. I'd been lying down on the skeleton of the boat as to not be observed by any passer-by.

Dustin touched my shoulder and I looked at him. His gold eyes were full of excitement; obviously, he enjoyed breaking the law. He stretched out his hand and I grabbed it.

"Welcome to my uncle's boat house," he said as he pulled me to my feet.

I looked around; it was small, with fishing gear lining the walls along with trophy fish such as a thirty-inch

Walleye. Uncle Ted tied the boat to a post near the front of the small waterway and closed the huge double doors that led out to the river. Light seeped in through the filthy windows on the wall, giving enough light to see where you were going, but not enough to make out much detail. The scent of river water and fish guts permeated the air, but I didn't mind, I was used to the smell from fishing trips with my dad.

My stomach twisted. I was never going to get to do that with my dad again.

"It isn't as easy as you thought it would be, is it?" Uncle Ted said as he hung his fishing gear on the wall.

I shook my head. "No, it isn't. I keep thinking about how things had been before, and how they won't be like that again."

Dustin put his arm around me. "Hey, your dad will put your mom straight, just give it some time."

"Yeah, unless she decides to have him admitted as well," I replied gloomily.

Seconds after the words left my mouth, there was a knock at the land entrance of the boat house.

CHAPTER NINE:

"Someone's here," Uncle Ted said, starting to walk towards the door.

I gave Dustin a horrified glance. He picked me off my feet and lowered me into the cold river water. "Hide under the wooden dock ledge, they won't be able to see you, we don't have any electricity in here," he whispered.

Nodding, I slipped under the dock and held onto one of the support beams. Already, my day seemed to be nothing but an endless game of cat-and-mouse, in which the mouse, being me, never had enough time to run.

I listened as the door opened and Uncle Ted greeted the two new guests.

"Hello, you must be Theodore Tomsworth, my name is Detective Roland, and this is my partner, Detective Myers. We'd like to ask your nephew a few questions."

Crap. The two detectives from the hospital were here already? Man, those crazy bin people sure did not like being outwitted by a seventeen-year-old who was just on her deathbed.

"Dustin! What did you do this time?" Uncle Ted called, playing the part of the annoyed guardian. "You know I have to leave on a business trip in a few hours!"

"Whatever it is you think I did, I didn't," Dustin told the detectives, walking towards them. I assume he was shaking his head in false retaliation.

"We're not here to accuse you of anything," replied Myers with a hint of suspicion, "we just want to know if you've been in contact with Matilda Blake."

"Mimi? No, not since last night," Dustin replied. "Why, is she okay?"

"She's missing," answered Roland.

"Missing, how?!" Dustin demanded. If I didn't know better, I would have believed his act. "It wasn't the—"

"No, she jumped out the window," Roland quickly said as to prevent Dustin from freaking out further.

"Then how is she missing?" Dustin demanded.

"As you know, your friend is in a fragile mental state and—" Myers began but Dustin cut him off.

"No, she's not. I talked to her last night. She's upset, yes, but I would not call her state of mind fragile." Dustin's voice was dangerous, and I knew that his stare was daggers as well.

"So, you haven't talked with her since last night?"

"No, we sort of had a falling out."

"A falling out?" repeated Roland.

"An argument, a fight, it ended with me leaving, alright?!" Dustin's temper soared.

"Then you don't mind if we have a look around your boat house?" Myers said.

"No, by all means," said Uncle Ted. "Just find the poor girl."

Footsteps sounded and I barely breathed. The footsteps grew louder as they approached me, and I sank deeper into the water. My limbs were numb, and I knew I couldn't keep up the silent breathing much longer, nor could I remain in the water. If the cops didn't get me, the fish sure would.

I smiled grimly; look at how far I'd come in a week. From pushing up daisies to sleeping with the fishes. The death metaphors couldn't have gotten more cliché.

The footsteps stopped right above my head.

My heart quickened; he saw the ripples; he knew I was there. Silently, I took a deep breath then submerged below the surface, holding onto the beam to stay under without making any waves.

A beam of light shined above me and I knew I had made the right decision. It stayed there for a couple of seconds, but to me, it felt like a lifetime. When the beam disappeared, I remained submerged, fearing that it was only feigning and hoping that I'd resurface to be caught. It didn't. I counted to fifty before going up for air.

It was hard, but I forced myself not to gasp when I resurfaced, and I'm lucky I did because Roland was right above me.

"—been a fish," he said as he pushed himself to his feet. "But it's hard to tell, the river is so filthy."

"You're probably right," agreed Myers.

"Besides," Roland continued as if Myers hadn't said anything, "nobody is that quiet, especially not somebody in as weak of state as her. And the water is too cold for anybody to stand. They'd die of hypothermia pretty quickly."

Myers didn't comment.

"So, what'd you think about what the kid said?" asked Roland. I was getting the impression that he was the awkward talking type.

"He's lying through his teeth. She's been in contact with him and he knows where she's heading. He knows more than he'll ever reveal to us," replied Myers, obviously bored of Roland's pointless questions.

"I don't mean about whether he's lying, I mean about whether the girl's sane."

"Don't go thinking about that," Myers told him. "It's best to stay out of Sandra Blake's business, she's the best lawyer around. She can have us neck deep in legal complaints if we go questioning her judgment. Besides, even if the girl's sane, and her mother is just being paranoid, we have other problems to worry about."

"Like our serial killer who targeted her."

Myer's didn't respond.

"She shouldn't be out right now; she doesn't realize just how much danger she's in."

"She's young," Myers said, choosing his words carefully. "She's also traumatized. Matilda Blake knows what tried to kill her, and she's scared. She's either hiding from it, or out hunting it. Either way, it's our job to find her before something horrible happens to her."

There was silence as they continued searching the boat house, then, "You know, in all my years as a detective, I've never heard anyone refer to a serial killer as an 'it.'"

Myers sighed. "Do you ever stop talking?"

"Not really."

"Would you shut up?"

"Not until you've answered my question."

"What question?"

"This town, what's so strange about this town? I've been here six months and already I've encountered more obstacles than I ever did in Chicago. Not only with the suicide angle, but also now with the serial killer angle. Do you not believe in serial killers or suicides? What's going on here?" Roland demanded.

Myers must have been contemplating telling him what was wrong with this town for a long time before Roland asked. It's not an easy answer.

"This town is different, and unlike the big city, we're secluded in what remains of the wild. Most people believe that it's because of state and national forestry, but here, we know it's something much different. It's what remains of the ancient wilderness. You may not understand it now, and you may laugh at our superstitions, and I hope to God you're right, but one day, you will understand why we're weary when it comes to truth and reality versus want and illusion."

"That wasn't an explanation."

"It's all that I can give."

Roland realized that Myers had given him all the explanation he was going to get. "She's not here." He sighed, taking a few steps away from the water.

"Let's get out of here, this place gives me the creeps."

I listened as they walked out the door and left, completely unaware that I had been right under their noses. But one thing was for sure, they had pinned Dustin. Maybe he didn't look as convincing as he sounded. It wouldn't be long before they came back knocking.

Slowly, I counted to fifty, just to make sure that the Detectives wouldn't double back. I was frozen; my limbs stiff and my skin numb to the point that I couldn't feel it. My teeth began to chatter uncontrollably, and I knew if I was in the water any longer, I would drown or die of hypothermia. I hit fifty and reached up for the dock, curling my fingers around the edge, then attempted to pull myself out of the water.

My muscles froze.

I couldn't move; I was stuck halfway out of the water.

"Come on," I muttered to myself, "just another foot; you're almost there." But my muscles didn't listen. The grip I had on the dock was slipping; it was only a matter of time before I splashed back into the freezing water.

You're probably wondering how the river was so cold even though it was June. Well, the river water comes from a series of natural springs about a mile north of town. The springs are ice cold, so the river never warms up this far up. Hell, I don't think it ever warms up.

The dock slipped out of my grip, and I splashed back into the icy water. I fumbled as I tried to resurface, momentarily confused as to which way was up and which way was down.

I was at the end of my rope.

Cold, that was the only thing I felt I knew. I was cold, so cold. There was no way of getting rid of it, no way of warming up. I gasped in a breath of air and choked on the icy water that came with it. My lungs burned, sending tears to my eyes. I was so tired, all the energy gone, spent up trying to hide. I failed. My reward: death.

My body gave up on me, no longer able to stay above the surface.

The door of the boat house opened.

"Help!" I screamed, not caring who it was. I couldn't die, not now. If I spent the rest of my life in a crazy bin, then to hell with it because dying here would be worse. "Hel—" I was pulled under.

It wasn't just my muscles keeping me under, something grabbed me, pulling me under, trying to drown me. I began to panic, flailing my arms in an attempt to escape, but it was useless. I sucked water into my lungs, no longer able to hold my breath.

My lungs were burning worse than ever. Whoever said drowning was peaceful never experienced it. It's the most frightening feeling in the world. All you want to do is breathe, but every time you try, you suck in more water, and your lungs burn worse, and the panic increases, causing you to breathe more. I thought I was a goner.

The next thing I knew, I was spewing my guts out on the dock, gasping the air back into my lungs. My lungs still burned, but it wasn't the same intensity as before. I was shaking from head to toe, the cold not going away even though I'd managed to escape my soggy prison.

I looked around for my savior and felt my heart rate drop slightly upon seeing Dustin, drenched from head to toe, his brown hair soaking wet and turned to an almost black color. He'd taken his shirt off, revealing a nicely toned eight pack he neglected to mention. I hated myself for staring, but I just couldn't get myself to stop. There were awkward pink and white stripes that took up about twenty percent of his stomach and chest, but I dismissed them as marks from rubbing up against the dock as he pulled me out. However attractive I found him before, he was even more so now. He knelt above me with a look of relief written across his face. I guess I wasn't the only one who thought I'd die.

"S-s-since w-w-when d-d-d-d-do you k-n-n-now CPR?" I asked him through chattering teeth.

He raised both his brows. I kind of wished he would quit trying to only raise one. "Once again, I save your life, and you ask the most stupid question that comes to your mind?"

"C-c-can't help-p-p it-t-t," I replied. "My br-r-rain d-d-doesn't w-w-work-k-k right-t-t-t when it-t's c-c-c-cold-d-d."

His expression softened and he pulled me into his arms. "I thought I told you to quit trying to die on me," he said softly in my ear. He was so warm, even after his swim in the river to fish me out.

I cuddled closer to him, not caring about what he was thinking. Warm, I wanted to be warm. Dustin was warm. Simple solution: steal all the heat from Dustin.

He reached over and grabbed his grey hoodie and pulled it over me. It was warm and smelled like him. I inhaled deeply and closed my eyes; I was so tired that I was ready to fall asleep right there.

"Hey, you need to stay awake just a little longer, Mimi," he said, rising to his feet and scooping me up into his arms. For an instant, I remembered the first time he scooped me up into his arms. How I hated him at the time. To think that now I had fallen for him, I'm sure I would have vomited if the thought had crossed my mind then.

"W-where a-r-re the d-d-de-t-tec-t-tives?" I stuttered.

"Gone," he answered. "I made sure they'd driven away before I came to the boat house. God, I wish I would have been a little faster."

"I'm al-l-live aren't-t-t I?" I said, trying to get him to stop feeling guilty. Dustin has saved my life countless times. Well, he also nearly got me killed multiple times too.

"Yes, but you nearly drowned and you're dying of hypothermia. Your lips are purple, Meems."

I reached up and touched my lips; they felt just as numb as the rest of me.

Dustin pushed the door open, and I was blinded by the light. My eyes had grown accustom to the dimness of the boathouse, so the sunlight hurt.

I shaded my eyes and squinted at the perfectly trimmed green lawn and gigantic garden with, was that a cupid fountain?

My jaw dropped. Tomsworth; that was his uncle's name. Tomsworth, as in the billionaire who lived in the huge estate just south of town. I had heard rumors about this place: the house was said to be the size of a palace, and there was no disappointment there. Two turrets towered above the treetops, giving the mansion the feeling of a castle. It was built of huge stones, adding to the medieval feeling of the place, and it had to be at least five, maybe seven, times larger than my own home, and my house is huge. It didn't just look like a castle; it really was one.

"Y-y-y-you l-l-live here?" I asked in awe, staring up at the beautiful white marble archway Dustin had just walked through.

"Yes, with my uncle," he replied casually. I could see him trying to conceal the grin.

"B-b-b-but—"

"I said that my parents' house wasn't big, not that my uncle's house wasn't," he cut me off, knowing what I was going to say. "And besides, Uncle Ted doesn't have an indoor theater room."

I glowered at him as he opened the door to his Uncle's house, entering the grand foyer. Surprisingly, it was bright, unlike its gloomy exterior, with a modern theme to it. There was still a grand white marble staircase branching off to the upper floors, but you could see the modern styles in architecture and furniture. I half expected a mob of maids to come running to our aid. On the ceiling was a glass dome with sunlight falling through it like a waterfall, the droplets hitting the orbs on the crystal chandelier, creating rainbows that filled the room with a sea of color.

Dustin didn't bother looking around, already bored of the grand décor that he'd seen every day since he'd moved here. Instead, he clambered two stairs at a time up the marble steps, veering off to the left down a hallway with suits of armor lining it on either side, then to a small maple door. He opened it, then began to climb the narrow stone swirling staircase. His room was in one of the two turrets. We reached the top of the staircase, and he pushed the trapdoor up, lifting me onto the floor above before crawling up himself.

"Welcome to my home," he said, spreading his arms wide to gesture at the small living quarters he'd acquired.

Somehow, he'd managed to get a full-sized bed up into the circular room, along with a large, curved dresser and wardrobe. A huge bay window covered a fourth the wall, giving the perfect view of the garden below and the river and forests beyond.

He had the best room in the house.

"I know it isn't much, but I like it," he said as I let it all soak in.

"It-t-t-t's p-p-p-perfec-c-ct," I managed, giving him a weak smile.

He smiled back. "Not what you expected is it?"

I shook my head.

"Uncle Ted wanted me to stay in one of the larger rooms downstairs, but I thought this one was the right choice for me. I'm not a fan of wide-open spaces. I didn't have that much stuff when I moved up here from Chicago, so if I had chosen one of the rooms he wanted me to have, it would have been virtually empty." He closed the trapdoor then turned back to me. "Let's get you out of those soaking clothes and into something warmer, shall we?"

I began to blush.

"What is it?" he asked.

"I d-d-doubt-t-t you hav-v-ve an-n-n-nyth-th thing."

Dustin began to laugh. "You can't stay in those clothes, Mimi, you'll freeze to death. I'll get them dry and back to you, along with the rest of your stuff, but for now, I have a couple of things you can wear of mine that I've never worn." As he spoke, he walked over to his dresser and dug through until he pulled out a pair of sweats and sweatshirt that looked brand new. He handed them to me, then waited as I sat, blushing even deeper.

"Uh, D-d-d-dust-t-tin," I stuttered.

"Mmm?"

"G-go aw-w-way."

"Oh!" He realized that I wasn't comfortable stripping in front of him. "I'll just be, you know, um, knock on the trapdoor when you're done." He then lifted the trapdoor and fled through it, trying to hide his embarrassment.

I rolled my eyes and started stripping off the wet clothes. The fact that he hadn't thought of that on his own bothered me. What a guy.

As I slipped on the sweatpants and sweatshirt, I felt slightly warmer, no longer shivering so violently. I put my teeth chattering under control and rolled my wet clothes into a ball. Then, I decided not to knock on the trapdoor, but instead to investigate the room a little further, you know, just to see what he had hiding.

The first thing I did was go to the wardrobe. Nobody has a wardrobe now-a-days and I wanted to see if he actually kept anything in there. I opened it and found a suit, jacket, and snow-pants hanging. Virtually empty, as expected. But why was it so wide?

I began tapping on the wood at the bottom, and found, to my surprise, that it was hollow. Upon closer examination, I found a space just wide enough to fit my finger through. The wood was only an inch thick. I hooked my finger then lifted; the wood came out easily.

"So, you couldn't help but figure I had an escape route hidden in my room?" Dustin's voice came from behind me.

I yelped, dropping the board while hitting my head on the wooden frame of the wardrobe.

Dustin walked over and gently lifted me away from the wardrobe. "It's alright, I was going to show it to you anyways."

"Th-that's the r-real reason y-you chose this r-r-room?" I said, figuring I was right.

"Yeah, it is. That way, if I ever get cornered up here, I have a way to escape, and now, so do you." He put me down on his bed and threw a pile of blankets on me.

I began to shiver uncontrollably again as the cold radiated around me under the blankets, and it didn't go unnoticed by Dustin.

"Just hold on a second, Meems," he said, running to his drawers. "I gotta put on something dry, then I can help you warm up."

I closed my eyes and continued to shiver. The dry clothes and blankets could only do so much. I was cold, lacking completely of warmth. What I needed was something warm.

"Mimi, stay awake now," Dustin said, shaking me suddenly.

My eyes were so heavy, but I forced them open. His face was so soft with worry, with concern. I stared into his golden eyes, and I felt myself losing focus.

"No, you keep looking at me, don't you dare fall asleep!" He was panicking now.

"I'm s-s-so t-t-tired," I stuttered, closing my eyes once more.

"Mimi, you have to stay awake, just until you've warmed up," Dustin insisted, shaking me again. "If you don't, you might not wake up ever."

I understood what he was trying to do, but I couldn't keep my eyes open. It was as if someone was putting bricks on them. "Dustin, I-I-I'm so c-c-cold."

He slipped in next to me, his body like a portable heater. He wrapped his arms around me and pulled me close to his chest. "I know, just keep your eyes open."

I tried to do as he said, but my weariness won out. I was already running on empty, even before I'd gone in the water. It was a miracle that I wasn't already dead. For all I knew, I should have been sleeping with the fishes at that moment, gone with that invisible force that was pulling me under. It was probably some anguished soul who drowned in the river long ago, hoping that I would make for a good companion to share in its miserable afterlife.

Stay awake. Easy for Dustin to say, he wasn't the one who'd nearly died twice in the past week. He wasn't the one who was on the run because his mom couldn't accept the truth about him, who had lost the entirety of his past life because of one single mistake.

Or maybe I was the one being selfish.

Dustin had lost everything. I'd known him just over two months and was only now discovering that his parents were dead, that he'd been living with this Uncle he hardly spoke to. He'd given up his entire life to come here, to this small town, because he didn't have anywhere to go. He was an orphan, a friendless orphan, and he had sought me out.

Why would he do that?

I shivered up against his chest, trying to stay awake. What was the point? This was the third way I almost died. The poison had failed, and so had the river, but the cold; it just might succeed. The demon just might get my soul after all.

There was something I was missing, some piece of information that I just couldn't recall. It was hanging out in front of me, like a carrot on a stick, dangling just out of reach, taunting me. If only I could manage to grasp it, then everything would make sense.

But what was I missing?

My mind went back to the beginning of it all: Jenny's death.

It had started out as any other day would. I got up, got dressed, ate breakfast, and went to school. There were rumors of a new kid in town; whispers I heard in the halls at school, but it wasn't anything concrete. Just something about some kid from Chicago. Jenny, of course, was all over them, being the gossip queen that she is. She went around all day, digging up as much as she could get her hands on about who the new kid was, and what was the new kid like? Was it a he? Was it a she? Tall, short, fat, skinny, blonde, brunette, blue eyes, brown eyes? She'd been able to fish out a gender and an address, but that was about it.

The second Charlie found out that she wanted to go stalk the new kid, he became jealous. By that point, he knew the new kid was a guy, and he couldn't stand that Jenny was interested in meeting him. He thought she was being unfaithful.

That's what led to the fight.

Jenny couldn't handle the fact that Charlie didn't trust her. She screamed at him, calling him just about every name in the book. Charlie retaliated back, telling her to "go to hell" before he stormed out. It was the last thing he ever said to her.

I was left alone with Jenny. She still insisted that we go and find out who the new kid was, maybe ask him to hang out. I knew her ploy; she was intent on getting me to break up with Teddy. Things had gotten rocky between us, and that was before I found out that he cheated on me with Trisha. I was so oblivious, and Jenny didn't have the heart to tell me, to break my heart.

She never gave me the address.

Jenny left after I refused to go with her.

About five minutes later, Jenny called me. Her voice was weak, and I thought she was trying to pull one over on me. It wasn't until I heard the sickening crunch that I realized that she wasn't faking, she was actually dying. I ran to my car, still talking to Jenny. I told her to hang on, that I was coming, and that help was on the way.

I arrived at the scene of the crash in less than three minutes.

Her car had hit a telephone pole, after she had slipped on a patch of ice that had escaped the spring thaw, and it had completely destroyed the cab. Blood was everywhere, all over the grass, all over the wreckage of the car and the telephone pole. Then, I saw her mutilated body, her head slumped over the steering wheel, her eyes still wide open. The airbags hadn't deployed. I ran to her, in an attempt to help her, when I realized she was already dead. She had died upon impact. I'd been talking to a dead audience on the phone.

I began to call out her name, softly at first, then louder as the denial kicked in. I reached out and began shaking her, trying to get her to respond, my brain not accepting the fact that she never would respond again.

Sirens wailed as the police and ambulance finally arrived.

The first responders had to rip me away from Jennifer. I couldn't leave her side, not when I had failed her, not when the one in the car should have been me. If I had just agreed to go with her, then maybe I could have stopped her death. At the time, I thought she'd taken it herself. Now, I knew it was the demon who'd done so.

They brought me to the ambulance and put a blanket around my shoulders, then someone washed away her blood. At that point, I was completely catatonic.

Someone called her parents, and my parents, who called Charlie. Charlie was the first to arrive, and he just about lost it when he watched them pry Jenny out of the car. Her body had been torn in half at the waist, and they had to take it out one piece at a time. Charlie couldn't watch, but I couldn't stop watching. I couldn't take my eyes off them as they worked, removing her remains from that crumpled up car. They put her in a body bag and wheeled it on a stretcher towards the County Medical Examiner's van.

That's when her parents arrived. I watched as her parents ran up to the police tape blocking off the crash site. It looked like half the town was there, watching the horror unfold. They weren't allowed to come over, like Charlie had been, but they saw me, and they hated me. I listened as they yelled curses at me, blaming me for Jenny's death. One of the officers tried to explain that I had been the first responder; that Jenny had driven in the car alone, that I had done everything I could. They didn't care. Their baby was gone; never coming back. It was just as much my fault as it was hers.

Soon after, my dad arrived to take me home. He gave my keys to an old friend of his that he had brought along, then he drove me home and brought me up to my room, all in silence. He knew better than to try and say something. There was nothing to be said. Instead, he let me wear out my sorrows, my self-loathing, and my pain.

Teddy came over a little later that day. I was still in shock, so when I opened the door, it didn't register that it was him. He still had his piercings, and his hair was long and shaggy. When he saw me, the hollow shell that I'd become, he almost went back on his plans, he almost pulled me into his arms and consoled me. He almost cared about me.

But he didn't.

He broke my heart instead. Told me that he was breaking up with me because he'd found someone better, more attractive, more blah, blah, blah.

It was one of the darkest moments of my life.

When I returned into the house, I walked straight to the kitchen and opened the knife drawer. I pulled out the big, long chopping knife and went up to my room. I was going to end it, to put a stopper on all my pain.

I walked into my room and locked the door.

That's when Jenny first appeared to me. She was raw energy at that time, explosive and dangerous, but she'd been watching me since I arrived at the crash site. Jenny had watched everything, seen all the things that I had been through, and saw how I had given up. She talked me out of cutting myself, somehow convincing me that there was a light in the darkness; that everything was going to be alright.

But never once did I see that demon.

Maybe Dustin was right after all. Maybe the demon was trying to kill everyone who got close to him. But why? Why go after Dustin of all people?

And why Jenny? Why choose Jennifer Goodridge of all people?

There had to be a connection, something that made everything fit.

The only thing I could come up with was me. It made some sense; the demon had chosen to show itself to me in the halls of school, not Dustin. The demon had gone after me. It tried to kill me. But it hadn't shown up until after I met Dustin.

So then back to Dustin. Why was the demon going after Dustin? There had to be a reason; demons don't randomly target people. They need a reason. What was that reason?

Why do I care? Who cares whether a demon had a reason for going after someone? Did it really matter? Did staying awake any longer and worrying about problems even make a difference? I should just give up, embrace the inevitable.

I found myself realizing that it did matter as I drifted off into the blank world of unconsciousness.

CHAPTER TEN:

I resurfaced into the land of consciousness, and discovered I'd been moved. I was no longer in Dustin's small circular room, rather, I was buried under a thick quilt in a larger, rectangular room with large windows that gazed over the backyard garden. Late twilight streamed in the window, encompassing my surroundings in a faded orange light.

Lifting the quilt off, I was hit by a wave of cool air, causing me to shiver. I draped the quilt back over my shoulders and swung my legs down onto the cool wood floor.

I wasn't home.

Truthfully, I'd been hoping that this all had been a bad dream. I never imagined that my life could turn inside out like it had over that past—how long had I been out? A few hours, a day, a week? My stomach growled. I guessed anywhere from a couple hours to a day.

Come on, Matilda, I told myself, *don't give up now, you've finally hit a safe spot.* Considering what I'd been through, waking up in a soft bed that wasn't my own wasn't exactly the worst thing that had happened to me.

I bit my lip.

How many times in the last week had I nearly died? Maybe getting out of bed wasn't such a great idea.

I shrugged. When have I ever listened to myself? I had a chance a few months ago to not step down the path I'd chosen, and now it was too late. I'd already begun my descent to hell.

My toes inched themselves forwards as I slipped my weight onto my feet. I wobbled slightly, but I took that as a good sign. Hopefully, that meant that I was still alive.

Slowly, I took a few steps forwards, feeling my way across the cool wood flooring and towards the hard-oak door. The room was modern and bright, with a metal desk on the far wall, and a curved mirror on the wall by the window. I just happened to glance in it and saw how awful I looked.

Over the past week, I'd been avoiding mirrors, fearing my reflection. My fears had not been in vain. I'd lost weight, more than should have been possible to lose in a week. Not only that, but my skin had become a sickly pale color, the color of a corpse. My hair was ratty and unkempt, and my eyes looked bloodshot.

The poison still had a hold on me, I still hadn't been cured.

I wanted to cry; that's why Dustin had insisted I stay in the hospital, he saw that I was dying, and he wanted me to be comfortable. God, I'm such an idiot. Of course, modern medicine didn't know how to cure demonic poison, how would it? It wasn't like modern medicine consisted of any medieval practices. The dark ages had been pushed into the corner like the people then had just been a bunch of terrified superstitious lunatics that didn't know anything about the world. They didn't know that draining me of the infected blood was what needed to be done. No, the doctors had saved me from dying that day, but they couldn't stop the inevitable doom that was hanging over my head.

I wondered if my mother could see it.

Maybe Mom did know something was up, and maybe she'd called the Blue House just to check up on me. A shiver went down my spine. No, she did it because she heard me speaking to Jennifer a week after I nearly died. She thought I went off the deep end. Mom had been the one to knock at my door, then thought it better not to confront me about it, and instead, call the people at the loony bin to sort out her problem for her.

My knees became weak under me and I allowed myself to crumble to the floor. I was drained, exhausted, and barely functional. My life's light was dimming in my eyes; I probably had less than a week if I were to continue on without any treatment. Everything I tried was spent. The demon was going to win this round, and I still didn't have the slightest idea as to what was going on.

Or did I?

Hadn't Charlie accused me of being a demon when I first discovered the library? And in the car, he wanted to know my game plan, and scolded me for not coming up with a better one. My mind drifted back; he just knew, he always knew. Whenever I needed him, he just showed up in his beat-up Chevy as if by coincidence. Just the sheer number of times this happened should have been enough to tip me off that this was no mere coincidence, but I'd never thought anything of it until now.

No, there was something different about Charlie. Good or bad, I couldn't be completely sure of, but I was going to have a long talk with him the next time we met. That I was sure.

There was a prolonged growl that emerged from the region of my abdomen, and I figured that in order to survive, I was going to have to tame it. Mustering up some of the strength I had regained, I pushed myself to my feet and headed for the oak door. My mind was still swimming with all the problems I was facing when I heard a sound coming from just outside the window.

I paused.

Should I go investigate? Indulge my inner curiosity for a few moments, or should I leave it where it stood. The growling inside suggested I leave it where it stood, but, being the callous buccaneer that I am, I ignored that instinct and went to investigate.

I arrived at the window and gazed down at the marvelous gardens that spread out over the grounds like a festive cookie sweetening up the gloom of the boring gray platter upon which it lay. Down, closer to the edge of the gardens, near one of the many fountains, stood a solitary figure, glaring up at me.

My blood ran cold.

Though I couldn't make out any distinct features, I knew it was the demon glaring up at me, waiting for me to come out and play. It didn't take any steps forwards, rather, it stayed put, continuing to stare at me, like a crocodile stares at the antelope taking its long-deserved drink from the watering hole, noticing for the first time that it's trek had taken a deadly turn.

It was beckoning me, egging me to go join it. I could feel it in my blood, that burning desire to join it, to follow it, to be lost, to do the wrong thing.

I forced myself away from the window, sickened by my own desire. The demon hadn't poisoned me to kill me, no, it had wanted me to live. It wanted me to become ill, to fall victim to its horrid nature, to become infatuated with it. As long as I was infected, the demon would have its hold on me. Nowhere in heaven or on earth was I safe. This is what I get for missing church last Sunday.

I reached up and touched the locket strung around my neck; Jenny was going to kill me for how long she'd been in there, but I wasn't sure now would be the time to let her out again.

There was a squeak, and the iron handle doorknob began to twist. The black iron hinges squealed in protest as they were forced to swing open, revealing a refreshed Dustin in his favorite grey hoodie; his hair looked clean and ruffled, as if he'd run his hands through it more than once due to anxiety. He had dark rings under his eyes that hadn't been there before, so I figured he hadn't slept since I last saw him. His golden eyes swept across the bed, and horror filled them upon seeing it empty. He took a step, then his eyes fell upon me, standing with my back to the window.

"Mimi, you're awake and up!" he exclaimed in pure relief.

I smiled weakly at him. "How long was I gone?"

"Only a day and a half. I had to carry you down to one of the guest rooms so I could sleep, not that it mattered though, I was going to have to move you soon anyways."

"How come?"

"The detectives are getting a search warrant for this property. They know you're here."

I opened my mouth, then closed it. It had already occurred to me that the detectives weren't fooled by

Dustin's performance yesterday, I had heard them discussing how awful it was.

"It's too bad Uncle Ted left yesterday on his 'business' trip, so they'll have to go through me to get in here." Dustin smiled wryly at the thought.

"You must be the worst actor in the history of worst actors for them not to believe your gag yesterday," I recounted, returning the smile.

"I am," he replied, holding out his hand. "But that's beyond the point. Right now, we need to get you ready to leave. They'll be here very soon, and I'm sure you'd rather be wearing your own clothes, and not my sweats, when they arrive."

I looked down at my clothes and agreed, I hated wearing baggy clothing; it made me look fat. Taking his hand, he led me out of the guest room and into the hallway, away from the glowering eyes of the demon.

CHAPTER ELEVEN:

After a good shower, meal, and a change of clothes, I was feeling one hundred percent better than when I first awoke. The simple amenities of life do wonders for the body.

Dustin had returned my survival pack to me, packed with new food that would last longer than a week, along with some other provisions that I hadn't originally thought about, including deodorant, salt, and a flask of holy water. I pulled my hair back into a braid that swung halfway down my back, and donned a black windbreaker that Dustin lent me. When night fell, I was going to crawl into the back of Dustin's Cadillac De Vil and he was going to drive me out to the cemetery so I could spend a few nights in the library. We figured Charlie would make his rounds and come across me, then he would help me from there to take the heat off Dustin for a little while.

All we had to do was beat the cops.

I sat in the majestic entry hall, staring up at the mural of the heavens painted upon the curving arches while I sat on the white marble stairs. One thing was for sure; Dustin's uncle had class. As I marveled at the mural, my mind began to wander. Maybe one day I would be among the stars in heaven. I may be Roman Catholic, but it doesn't mean that I know for sure what heaven will be like, and I prefer to think it's open to interpretation. Heaven could be the stars, each soul shining their light upon humanity, trying to guide each and every person on their journey through life. Or maybe Heaven is a city in the clouds with glass buildings and a crystal flowing river through its heart, where the streets are lined with lampposts that signify each stage of existence, from the beginning to the end, through time and eternity. It could even be a fruit farm, filled with overbearing fruit trees as far as the eye can see, and fields of flowers that are eternally in the height of their bloom, filling the air with the sweet scent of blossoms in the spring. It could be any of those things, or it could be none of them. That's what I love about it, you won't know until you get there, and even if you get there, how will you know?

My smile faded. At the rate my health was failing, I just might get to arrive there sooner than I imagined, if I was able to arrive there at all. I still had the demon to worry about.

The last of the sunlight filtered through the crystals of the glass chandelier before Dustin entered the foyer. He was still wearing his grey hoodie that he was overly fond of; it's just too bad that it doesn't get hot until mid-June most years. He had his keys in his hand, so I figured we were leaving. I climbed down the steps to meet him.

"You're looking better," he noted with a grin.

"Food and showers do wonders for the body," I replied, returning the grin.

"Are you sure you're going to be okay; I could just drive you to the church and see—"

"Dustin, Father Edward would call my mom, and then I would end up in the Blue House," I cut him off. "We discussed this, remember?"

"Mimi, I thought you believed in your religion," Dustin insisted, trying a different argument to get me to go to the priest.

"And I thought you didn't," I retorted, folding my arms over my chest and planting my feet firmly.

"Why don't you want to try, he could perform an exorcism, and we could blame your crazy actions on you being possessed?!"

"Dustin, I don't think you understand," I tried to explain. "In this day and age, the church doesn't believe in demons. They believe that the devil is in this world, but it's in temptation, not an actual metaphysical creature. Just like the rest of the world, the church doesn't believe in fairies, dryads, elves, ghosts, or demons. If I were to go to Father Edward and ask him to heal me of demon poison, he would call the Blue House and have me admitted himself!"

"You don't know that."

"I do know that."

"No, you don't!" Dustin exploded. "Mimi, you're dying! I can see it in your eyes, you can't keep fighting the poison that's coursing through your veins! You put on a brave face, but it's draining you. I beg you, please, let me take you to a priest."

I stared at him in silence. He was scared, scared for me, for my wellbeing, not for his own. Dustin wanted me to risk getting caught, rather than risk my own impending death, and I was too afraid to do it myself. What was the point of cheating death if I would get caught and end up killing myself in the crazy house? It was counter-productive, crazy. Then, I looked at my situation through his eyes; if I didn't do this, then I was damning myself. I would do the same thing in his situation.

"I'm scared Dustin," I finally admitted to him and to myself. "I don't know what the right thing to do is."

His features softened, and he pulled me into his arms. "I'm scared too," he admitted, "but I can't let that stop me from acting. If this turns out to be a bad idea, then at least we tried it. I'd rather not give up without trying every possible permutation and fail after we tried everything. There is a cure for you, Mimi, we just have to keep trying."

We stood there for a second, then I pulled away. "Well, if we're going to see a priest, we should do it right after eight o'clock mass tonight. That way, we're at least on holy ground and the demon can't make a surprise visit."

"Right." Dustin ran his hand through his hair and walked to the door. "Would you care to join me on a ride to church?"

I walked up behind him, standing just behind the hinges of the door.

Dustin pulled the door open, and was about to walk out when, "Uh, hello detectives, fancy seeing you here."

My heart just about stopped. I slipped closer to the wall, pressing my back up against it in a fruitless attempt to fall into it, becoming one with the wall. This could not be happening, this wasn't happening! Why did the detectives have to show up now?

"Cut the act, kid, we're on to you," replied detective Myers.

"Alright, then, do you have the search warrant, or are you wasting my time?" Dustin asked acidly.

"We couldn't get the warrant," admitted Roland.

"Figures," Dustin said under his breath.

"But we would like to ask you some questions, and we want answers—real answers—this time. So much as attempt to lie and I will arrest you for obstruction of justice," Myers growled.

"May we come in?" asked Roland in a more tempered manner.

"No, but you can walk out with me. You see, I'd rather not be late for church; Uncle would be mad if he found out I didn't attend."

"What did I say about you lying to us, kid?" Myers growled. I could see him through the crack between the door and the wall. He looked ready to strangle Dustin.

"I'm not lying, just bending the truth slightly, I really am heading to church," Dustin insisted, trying to force them to take a step back so he could lure them away from my hiding place.

"Your uncle wouldn't mind if you were late just this once," insisted Myers. "Unless you're hiding something on the other side of that door."

"You got me," Dustin replied. "Mimi Blake is standing right behind the door."

"Why I oughta—" Myers rolled up his sleeves, and Roland had to step between him and Dustin.

"Mr. Harper, we are only asking for a few minutes of your time, it isn't all that much to ask," Roland pleaded, trying to restrain Myers.

The irritating sensation of a sneeze began to form in my sinuses. Always, at the inopportune moment, I have to sneeze. I shoved my hand under my nose, trying to snuff it out.

"I would prefer not to. I don't like cops, I'm from Chicago, and kids who speak with cops are snitches, and bad things happen to snitches."

"Kid, don't—"

I sneezed.

Dustin tried to cover it up, and sneezed almost on top of mine, but Roland caught it.

"Step aside, kid," Roland said, taking a step forward.

Dustin stood tall, his hand falling upon the edge of the door. "I can't do that."

"I'll give you one chance; you move aside or— AAAGGGHHH!" Dustin slammed the door on his hand.

"Mimi, run. I'll hold them off," Dustin commanded me.

"But where am I—?"

"RUN!" He stood against the door, struggling to keep it shut.

I began to run up the steps, and veered to the left, trying to keep myself from running into the suits of armor that lined the hallway. I was out of breath by the time I reached the maple door at the end.

"Stop! Matilda! We want to help you!" Roland followed me up the stairs and was at the other end of the hall. Dustin's defense failed.

I threw the door open. "Then why are you chasing me?" I yelled as I slammed the door shut, locking it with the heavy bolt. Unsure of how long it would last, I forced myself to race up the steps, gasping for breath by the time I reached the top.

How was I going to keep running? They had me pinpointed, and Dustin—he must have been arrested by Myers, and I figured Myers was roughing him up. Roland was pounding on the door now; I could hear it from the top of the steps. Those locks weren't meant for that kind of force.

I pushed the trap door open, then crawled through, throwing the door close. Then, I ran to the wardrobe and lifted the bottom out. This was going to be my way out. My finger slid under the knob, and I pulled up the wood, surprised that it was so light. Beneath the wood was another trap door. I opened this door too and saw that there was a ladder leading down into the darkness.

Great, a dark, creepy tunnel.

Taking a steadying breath, I unzipped my bag and dug through it. There had to be a flashlight.

A crashing sound rang through the room. The door was down, time was up; I had to go.

Cursing, I zipped the pack and climbed into the wardrobe, closing the closet door, then replaced the false wood bottom. I closed the trapdoor last, engulfing myself in complete darkness. My heart rate climbed as I listened for detective Roland to break through the trapdoor. A sudden paralysis took over, and I was glued to the spot.

The trap door opened with a smack as the hardwood was thrown against the hardwood.

Come on, Matilda, you must go, now, I told myself.

As hard as it was, I somehow managed to pry my hand from the ladder, and then my foot, and lightly placed it on the next rung down. Then, I moved the other down. My muscles were tired from the running, and it took all the self-control I had not to tremble. I concentrated on moving my feet down one rung at a time. Thirty-two, thirty-three, thirty-four, I continued to count the rungs as I descended.

I hate the dark. The dark is full of the unknown, and I hate the unknown. Over the past few days, I'd been dealing with nothing but the unknown, and I was beginning to lose my temper. When I next met that demon, I was going to give him a piece of my mind, along with a flask of holy water.

Seventy-nine, eighty, eighty-one, my foot landed on the ground.

It was dark, like, really dark. Dark as in you can't see your hand on your face dark. I felt like I had just walked into the valley of darkness, and I was on my own.

No, I wasn't alone.

I began to say my favorite psalm, the one that my dad used to read to me before I went to sleep when I was a little kid. *"My shepherd is the Lord, for nothing shall I want. Green pastures are where I'm led to repose; near waters still and deep, God will refresh my soul. I am lead onward*

in ways true to his name. If I should walk one day into the vale of darkness, no evil shall I fear with God at my side."
My feet started walking down the pitch-black passage.

The fear began to melt away, I knew I wasn't alone, I realized that I was never alone. Someone had been looking out for me the entire time. I continued reciting the psalm.

I walked headfirst into the wall. Or was it a wall? I felt it, and found that it wasn't stone like the rest, but rather it was wood. I felt around for a handle, and found, to my delight, that there was one.

I pulled on it, and there was a creaking noise, followed by a blast of cool air. The door opened, revealing the dark woods beyond. I stepped out into the cool night air, glancing back to see where I had exited, and saw that the door led out on the edge of the garden, out of one of the stone walls. I tried not to think about it, because it made absolutely no sense, and instead I glanced back up at the house.

The lights were still on, meaning that the cops were still there, searching. Roland lost my trail. The cops had Dustin, and all I had was a backpack and newly planted hope.

The odds were completely against me.

For the first time since this entire nightmare began, I smiled at my standings. I was outnumbered, out resourced, out flanked, and wounded, but I had something that no one else had.

I began to walk, not into the woods, but instead, towards the mansion. The cops may have Dustin now, but they didn't know what they were dealing with.

I crossed under the marble arch, and into the courtyard before the huge mansion. There were rose bushes lining the drive. I didn't notice them when Dustin first carried me from the river, but now I could see them with all their beauty and their thorns. Ducking into the bushes, I forced myself to crawl to one of the windows so that I could glance in.

The moon had yet to rise, so it was nearly pitch-black outside, with the only light coming from the stars. Lucky for me, that would cause anybody looking out a window to only see a reflection of the room they're in. As long as I stayed far enough away from the window, they wouldn't see me.

As I approached the edge of light streaming out of one of the windows, a thought occurred to me; what would I see when I gazed in? What was the point of me coming back to the house and risking my capture? Why was I crawling through rose bushes to glance into a window? I wanted to answer that it was because I owed Dustin, that it was my turn to help him, but I knew that wasn't the answer. Something was drawing me back, and it wasn't Dustin.

The reason was on the other side of the glass.

Stopping just underneath the window frame on the outermost edge of the house, I decided to take my first peak. Slowly, I raised my head until I could peek in through the glass without being detected. Inside was what I assumed was the living room. Dustin had neglected to give me a tour of his home out of fear of "time wasting" so I only had my sense of deduction to go on. There was a plush red couch in the center, facing the outer wall of the house and the grand fireplace that wasn't lit. Red curtains hung down next to each of the large windows, and the floor was tiled with hardwood. There were a few easy chairs on either side of the couch, and heavy wood doors like the ones I'd seen all over the house as the entry. They were both closed.

Sitting upon the red couch, with his arms cuffed behind his back, sat Dustin. He looked calm, which was the exact opposite of how I expected him to look, sitting straight back, not leaning against the back of the couch. His eyes were closed; a smug smile strewn across his face. The cops would not be happy when they saw him. The room was empty except for him, so I took that as a sign that they still searched for me.

Taking the chance, I knocked on the window.

His eyes snapped open and began scanning the room until they fell upon the window where I stood, peering in. The calm expression faded and was replaced with disbelief, followed shortly by annoyance. He jumped to his feet, quickly crossing the room to the window to push it open slightly.

"Mimi, what are you still doing here?" he asked in an unamused voice.

"I have no idea," I replied honestly.

"You have to leave," he said, sliding the curtain slightly over the window to be sure that the detectives wouldn't see that it was open when they came in. "If they find—"

"Dustin, I know, but something keeps drawing me back, and I want to find out why," I replied, cutting him off. "Besides, I've already fooled them twice, who says that I can't fool them again?"

"Mimi, this is serious, you could get hurt."

"I just crawled through the rose bushes; I think I'm beyond hurt right now."

He shook his head and glanced at the doors. "They'll be coming in soon, and I don't want you here when they do. They might spot you."

"I'm not just going to leave you, Dustin," I told him, taking my backpack off my shoulder. "Besides, I think I have a paper clip in here. You do know how to pick locks, right?"

"Of course, I do," he replied curtly.

I pulled out the paper clip and straightened one end into a pick, then placed it in his right hand. "Be quick, I want to get out of here."

Dustin was about to respond when the doorknob began to twist. In a blink of an eye, Dustin was back on the couch sitting as if he'd never stood up in the first place, and I crouched down.

The door opened and in strolled detectives Roland and Myers with angered looks. I guess they hadn't found me. Dustin smiled as they walked in; his disrespect for law enforcement was widely known now.

"So, I'm going to assume you lost her," Dustin said as they pulled up chairs to face him. "You didn't actually think we didn't have an escape plan ready, did you?"

"Mr. Harper, you're in a lot of trouble, and you're not helping your case by helping Miss Blake run," Roland replied, trying to keep his manner formal.

"Sorry that I care about my friend's health. If she were admitted to the crazy house, she would take her own life.

I've seen it happen before, and I won't let it happen to her," Dustin replied, not taking any notice to Myers cracking his knuckles.

Why was Myers acting so out-of-character? I knew Myers quite well, actually; Mom worked with him on more than one occasion, and so I knew most of the law enforcement officers by name. Myers was a quiet guy, and quite gentle. The anger I saw in him, the violence, it was out of place.

"Where did she go, Mr. Harper?" Myers asked, his eyes fixed on Dustin.

"Out the window," Dustin replied, and Myers smacked him across the face.

"Myers!" Roland yelled, jumping to his feet.

"If we're going to get answers out of him, this is the only way. I know how kids like this work, I've dealt with my share of them. They're all the same. The only way they talk is if they get smacked around a bit," Myers replied, but he calmed down and sank back into his chair.

Dustin relaxed slightly; his arm had twitched slightly outwards, meaning that he had picked the lock, releasing the restraints around his wrists. He had to continue on like his arms were restrained or else there was no chance at escaping.

Roland settled back into his chair. "We've tried playing to your delusion, Mr. Harper, but now, it's time that you see reality for what it is."

"Delusions?" Dustin asked, not comprehending. "What are you talking about?"

I covered my mouth; I knew exactly what he meant. Roland was going to do the only thing he knew how to do: rationalize.

"You killed those people in Chicago and made it look like suicide," Myers replied.

Dustin's eyes became wide with horror. Of all the things that they could have thrown at him, he was least prepared for that. "You think I—oh my—oh God—no! You've got it wrong! I am not a killer!"

"It started simple, your dog, maybe stray cats around the neighborhood, but that wasn't enough, was it?"

"You're sick." Dustin glared at him; his hatred for law enforcement only reinforced.

Roland continued as if Dustin didn't interrupt. "The violence escalated to fights. There's some sealed records of you from the time right after your parents died. If we can get them unsealed, will we be surprised at what we find?"

"You are way off base on this one, Detective," Dustin growled.

"Your friend's dad is the one who sealed the record."

"Because I asked him to; I didn't want a-holes like you digging through them and coming to the sick conclusion you're at!" Dustin spat at him.

"I'm sure I could convince him to unseal them, after he finds out the truth about you." Roland wiped the spit from his blazer.

"And what is that? Why don't you explain further?" Dustin dared. His teeth clenched so tight I thought they might shatter.

Roland looked to Myers, who nodded. I guess Myers was in the mood to watch people explode or something.

"Killing animals wasn't enough for you; the anger of your parents' deaths, the fact that you nearly died, it ate away at you and the violence escalated to the homeless, the ones who no one would look for. You had a good system, until you felt the need to be recognized for your work. Soon, you went after anyone you could lay your hands on; people around your age that you could charm. The need to kill only intensified until it reached the point that you murdered your best friend and made it seem like a suicide," Roland's voice was flat, as if everything he was stating was known fact.

Dustin lost it. "I DID NOT KILL MY BEST FRIEND!" he exploded, attempting to stand up, but Myers pushed him back into his seat.

"Sit down, or I'll take out my revolver and put a round through your knee," he growled.

"I didn't kill my best friend," Dustin repeated, completely at a loss for words. His anger was spent and replaced with horror and disbelief. "I didn't kill my best friend."

"You didn't realize you were doing it, kid," Roland explained as if it were completely normal for someone to turn serial killer and go on a killing spree. "You were traumatized after the accident that killed your parents. Your dad drove off that bridge because he was depressed. He killed your mother and nearly killed you—"

"MY FATHER DID NOT COMMIT SUICIDE!" Dustin roared, again trying to rise but Myers pulled his revolver and forced him back down, holding him back against the couch. He struggled against the restraints, but Roland took that as a sign to continue.

"You feel guilty for their deaths; you feel like it's your fault that your dad lost his job and that your family was going to be evicted from your home. You feel like your father's choice for a double homicide-suicide was your fault, so you enact that guilt upon others in a psychotic episode. The first few lives were on accident, but the escalation—"

"Shut up!" Dustin yelled.

"It caused you to kill your best friend."

"I said, SHUT UP!"

"When you realized what you did, you set it up to look like a suicide, and came back, pretending like you only discovered the body."

"I didn't kill him!" Dustin closed his eyes and began to weep, the pain of having to remember what he saw haunted him, and the detective's words were only tearing the wounds deeper. He knew he was innocent, but no matter how much he told himself that, Dustin still felt guilty for his friend's death.

Dustin's reactions were enough to convince Roland that he had the right guy. No amount of explanation or pleading or anger would convince him otherwise. His story made sense too, and I found myself becoming sick with Dustin, almost believing that no demon existed, that the world could be as simple as a psychotic killer's rampage.

But I knew better. I'd seen the demon, face-to-face, and there's no drug out there good enough to do what the poison was doing to me.

The police got exactly what they wanted, a person who could take the blame.

Wait a second, they got exactly what they wanted: a perfect case tied neatly with a bow. That never happens.

"Your uncle took you in after the death of your friend, and you thought you could put your past behind you, but you couldn't. You kept having those episodes, and people continued to die," Roland continued, feeling the need to complete his theory. "First it was Jennifer Goodridge, a nice, pretty girl who had her whole life ahead of her. But her death wasn't satisfying; it reminded you too much of your parent's death, and it caused you to stop for a little, afraid someone might notice. That's when you saw Matilda."

Dustin opened his eyes; they were red and swollen from crying. He fixed them on Roland and dared him to continue, to say what I dreaded to hear.

"You fixated on her, tried to befriend her out of guilt. But that guilt wasn't strong enough, now was it? You had to try and killer her too!"

"I would never hurt Matilda!" Dustin said, his voice venomous.

"You drugged her, made her think she saw a new man at the café—"

"That's a lie!"

"—and when her ex walked out and saw her dying, you had to save her or else have your cover blown. You stayed at the hospital to make sure she didn't remember anything, and then you continued to drug her, to make her go mad."

"Matilda isn't mad!"

"You drove her to run, to have no one to trust. She's weak, and you planed on extorting her weakness, to take her out in a less public place, to make it look like she committed suicide, just like the others!"

"THAT'S ENOUGH!" Dustin screamed.

"You're a monster, Mr. Harper, there's nowhere left to hide. You planned on killing Miss Blake tonight and burying her body in a place only you could find, so you could come back and relive your fantasy, over and over." Roland became silent, his conjecture complete.

Dustin stared at him as if he were the most disdainful creature he had ever seen. "You sick, sadistic, lying, son of-a—"

Myers hit him across the face with the butt of his gun before he could finish. When he came for the second hit, Dustin ducked and missed the hit by less than an inch. His lip was split from the first smack he'd received from Myers earlier, and now there was blood running down from a jagged cut just above his brow.

At that moment, I knew something was wrong with Detective Myers, and Roland and Dustin knew it too.

Roland grabbed Myers' arm and forced him back. "Myers, what is wrong with you? Have you lost it? You can't go around beating up suspects; the court will discount any confession we get out of him!"

Myers turned, and for the first time since he entered the house, I saw his eyes. His pupils were dilated and unfocused and they seemed to draw me towards him. The sudden urge to make my presence known overcame me, and I had to force myself down into the rose bushes to blot it out with pain. I knew what was wrong with Myers; the piece of the puzzle that was missing.

Myers was possessed.

I had to warn Dustin; he needed to know what was happening. The demon had found a way into his house, and now Dustin and Detective Roland were in danger.

I was cornered; either I leave and save myself, or I stay and try to be a hero.

Digging through my bag, I pulled out the flask of holy water. *"Angel of God, my guardian near, for whom God's love, commits thee here. Ever this day, be at my side, to light, to guard, to rule, to guide, Amen,"* I prayed, then I did the stupidest thing I've ever done in my life.

I jumped through the open window.

I'm not sure who was more stunned; Dustin, Detective Roland, or the demon. Uncapping the flask, I rolled and bellowed, "Be gone, demon!" as I splashed the contents of the flask on Detective Myers.

Steam rose off Myers as he screamed in agony. He set his eyes on me, and I felt all the courage that led me to dive through the window disintegrate into nothingness.

So maybe angering a demon may not have been the best plan.

Dustin chose that moment to show that he unlocked the cuffs and jumped Myers, throwing his arms around his neck in a choke hold. "MIMI RUN!" he screamed as the possessed Myers began trying to buck him off like a bull.

I dug through my pack in search for other important demon-fighting implements that I had. All I found was salt.

Well, at least I had salt.

Myers threw Dustin across the room and he hit a bookshelf; it came toppling down on top of him.

"DUSTIN!" I cried, taking a step to reach him.

The demon stood in my path. "Ah, Matilda Blake, we meet again," it cooed.

I held the salt in one hand, and the flask in the other. There was still some holy water swishing around inside it, but I didn't want to use it all before I could trap it. "Get out!" I commanded it, holding up the flask of holy water. "You have no permission to be here."

It let out a horrid laugh. "My dear Mortuus Loquis, do you not realize that I am far more powerful than that? You cannot defeat me; darkness will always win out in the end, and soon you will be little more than a memory."

"Not if I can help it," I replied and tossed a bit more of my holy water on it. Quickly, before the demon could recover, I poured a circle of salt around it, and closed the circle, feeling a powerful surge of energy encompass the demon. It would be trapped as long as the circle remained closed.

The demon screamed in anger, pounding at the invisible energy walls of the prison that I had created around it. "I will not be trapped forever, Mortuus Loquis! I shall escape, and then I will come for your soul, and the soul of all those who you care about! You'll be my slave for all eternity."

"We'll see about that," I replied, then ran over to the bookshelf and began digging for Dustin. I tried to lift the shelf, but it was too heavy. I became distressed; being in the same room as a demon while your best friend has been trampled by a stampede of novels is not the best of situations.

Detective Roland recovered from his shock and looked from Myers to me. He didn't know what to do, and he didn't know what to think, and I didn't blame him; most of the time, I didn't know what was going on. He ran over and helped me lift the bookcase and lean it back against the wall.

Frantically, I began to dig for Dustin under the avalanche of hardcover novels and musty tomes. I found him, head bleeding, under a couple of outdated Oxford dictionaries. I checked his pulse, and found, to my relief, that it was still there. Though I was somewhat relieved, I still shivered, horrified by the thought of what happened to him.

"We need to get him out of here," I told Roland, attempting to keep my voice steady despite the demon yelling curses at me only a few meters away. "Will you help me?"

He nodded, still in shock. I put one of Dustin's arms around my neck and hoisted him up with Roland's help. Together, Roland and I carried an unconscious Dustin out of the room, leaving the demon hissing and throwing curses at us behind. We didn't have a lot of time before the demon escaped, but I couldn't do anything about that now. I had to worry about Dustin.

Roland and I carried him through the arching corridor, through the foyer, then out the front door and out into the courtyard before I dropped him. I was too tired to carry him any further.

My knees buckled and I collapsed onto the drive, gasping for breath. My veins burned as my body fell into an uncontrollable spasm, no doubt from the poison coursing through my veins. After a few seconds, I let out a groan and forced myself onto my knees, trying to keep myself from vomiting.

"What the hell is going on here!?" Roland exploded, dumping Dustin as he watched me writhe in pain. Only now had he began getting over his shock and approached the realm of disbelief.

"Nothing much," I groaned, forcing back what little food I had consumed earlier in the day. "Just a demon trying to steal my soul for reasons unknown."

"You aren't serious," Roland said, throwing his hands to his head as if it were trying to spin around like an owl's.

"I'm dead serious," I replied as the pain subsided. "Why do you think there have been so many 'suicides' in the past few months? You think it's the work of a serial killer whom you believe to be Dustin Harper, but in reality, serial killers don't exist. Killings like this are done by demons, and those possessed by demons. Serial killers are a result of the modern world trying to make sense of how such horrendous acts can be committed by people. I'm not the victim of a serial killer, just the next target of a demon." I pushed myself to my feet and tried lifting Dustin again.

"Demons don't exist," Roland insisted.

"Tell that to the one who's possessing your partner," I replied simply.

"But—"

"Look," I said, cutting him off, "you said it yourself the other day. Weird things happen in this town, and nobody will tell you what's going on. Well, that's because those who know are smart enough to keep their mouths shut, and those who don't know think you're crazy. Demons and ghosts exist, along with everything else that goes bump-in-the-night. You're not in the big city anymore, Detective. Welcome to Adams Grove, Michigan."

Roland looked at me as if I was crazy, but then chose to accept my explanation as fact. Besides, if I was in a fragile state of mind like my mom claimed, then I wouldn't have just jumped through a window and saved the lives of my accused serial killer friend and a detective out to bring me to the crazy house. Or maybe I would. Wow, maybe Mom is right, I am crazy.

I tried not to think about it while he helped me put Dustin into the back seat of his Cadillac De Vil. Dustin was too tall to fit perfectly in the back, so I had to bend him into an awkward position in order to close the door. As I tried to close the door, Roland took out his spare handcuffs and cuffed Dustin's wrist to the interior door handle.

"What are you doing?" I demanded.

"I'm not convinced that he doesn't have something to do with the murders. I'm not going to get jumped by a killer just because some kid with a mental condition says he's innocent."

My anger flared up. "I would have you know that I am completely, one-hundred percent capable of thinking clearly and undelusionally. Considering everything that I have been through in the past week, I probably have a better grasp on reality than reality itself! Just because you are unable to accept the reality of what you are seeing does not mean that I am crazy." I jammed him in the chest with my index finger just to prove my point. I had to bite back the pain of jamming my finger, but it was worth it.

Stupid adults, just because they're older does not mean that they have all the answers. The problem with age is that with experience comes results that close our minds to all answers, making us decide what we can consider to be probable and improbable. Age isn't an advantage, it's a burden on our free will. The more we think we know, the less we can come to know.

I climbed into the driver's seat and took the key from its hiding place in the visor and coaxed the engine to life. It roared and I felt some relief; at least something was working. Detective Roland climbed in the passenger's side of the car.

"Um, don't you have your own car?" I asked, trying not to sound offensive.

"I'm an officer of the law, and you are a run-away that I am charged to turn in," he replied. "You are now in my custody."

"Great, I save your life, and now I get admitted to the crazy house. Wonderful."

"I said that you're in my custody," Roland emphasized. "I never said I was going to turn you in."

I smiled at him. "So, what are you doing then, Detective?"

"I'm going to go where you go, and help you find a way to damn this demon back to hell so I can get my partner back. Then, I'm going to turn you in."

I clenched my teeth and glared at him. "You're awful, have you no morals?"

"There's a fine line we cops mustn't cross, and I plan on not crossing it," Roland replied. "However, if you were to somehow escape my custody, then I would have to search for you again."

I whistled. "Politics, you sound just like my mother."

"Your mother would send you to the Blue House if she were here."

"True." I pulled my locket out from under my shirt and opened it. Time that Jenny come out and tell me where I'd gone wrong in the past forty-eight hours.

Jenny materialized and stretched out her essence as I switched gears and began driving. "Jeez, I never thought I was going to get out of that—HOLY COP!" Jenny stared at Roland and then at me. "Aren't you running from the cops?"

"Yes, I am, where have you been for the last day?" I asked sarcastically.

"What?" Roland asked.

"He can't hear me, remember?"

"Nothing," I replied.

Jenny looked into the back seat and saw Dustin. "Wow, and you're killing your boy toy? See what happens when I get locked in a locket?! The first time this happened, you and Charlie went all psycho on each other, and now, you tried to kill Dustin, which I'm not so against." Then she noticed that his wrist was cuffed to the door. "Jeez, what kind of kinky business are you up to?"

I rolled my eyes and shook my head.

"What'd you open that locket for?" Roland asked, trying to ignore how awful my driving was.

"If I told you, you'd think I was crazy."

"You are crazy," moaned Dustin, sitting up in the back seat. There was dry blood matted in his brown hair and his pupils were slightly dilated, most likely because he had a concussion. "How many times have I told you books are instruments of torture?" He moved his hand but was cut short by the chain. For the first time since he became conscious, he noticed the cuff on his wrist. "You cuffed me to my car?"

"Glad you're alive," I said, turning onto Lake Street, near the cemetery.

"And I thought I told you to run," Dustin replied, looking up and noticing Roland for the first time. "Why did you cuff me to my car, and why do you have a cop in my car?"

"That's the question we all want answered," Jenny said, giving me an accusing smile.

"Detective Roland is helping me, I think," I answered.

"I am helping, as long as you keep your boyfriend on a leash," Roland replied.

"We're not dating," I said acidly.

"Right, I have a teenage son, I know hormones when I see them."

"OKAY!" Dustin said loudly. "Let's not get onto that subject! Mimi, where are you taking us, and why am I cuffed to my car?"

I turned through the third wrought iron gate of the ancient cemetery on the west side of town. "To the one place I know we can find answers to all our problems," I replied, pulling up to the old chapel and switching off the engine.

"The cemetery?" Roland asked skeptically.

"Yes, the cemetery," I confirmed. I climbed out of the car and opened the back door to assist Dustin.

Roland was there and un-cuffed Dustin from the door, but then re-cuffed him to his wrist.

Dustin glared at him. "You coppers are all the same distrustful, cynical, self-righteous a-holes."

Roland smiled at him. "I'm just making sure you don't make a run for it."

Dustin stared at him as if he just said, "I eat babies" and replied, "Where would I go? I'm injured, and even if I wasn't, there's no way in hell I would leave Matilda alone with you!"

"Boys!" I said loudly. "Knock it off!"

Dustin took a step, then fell onto his face, taking Roland down with him. "Stupid demon throwing me into a bookcase," he muttered angrily as I reached down to help him up.

I threw his arm over my shoulder and with the help of Roland, hoisted him back onto his feet. He saw the old red brick chapel looming before us, and he leaned closer to me.

"You can't take him here!" he whispered in my ear. "He's a normal! What if he drags the entire police department down here?!"

I laughed. "Like the department would believe him."

"He certainly believes you," Dustin replied moodily.

I sighed. "Dustin, he only believes me because he watched us take on a demon, one that is possessing his partner. I would believe me if I were him."

"Mimi, are you sure we can trust him?" Dustin insisted.

"Dustin Harold Harper, you are the last person who can lecture me on choosing who I can trust and who I can't!" I scowled and began to lead him into the chapel.

The chapel looked just the way it did the day Dustin showed me the library beneath it. The wooden crucifix still hung down from the rafters over the gray granite altar, and the room was dark. Roland pulled out his flashlight and switched it on.

"This room looks empty, as if it has been for a long time," Roland remarked, not understanding why I bothered coming to the chapel.

"That's the way it's supposed to look," Dustin told him as I helped him hobble in. "If it looked suspicious, the normals like you would have discovered its significance long ago."

"Normals? Are you saying you're not normal?" Roland asked, raising his eyebrow.

"Of course I am, do I seem all that normal?"

"Quit being a jerk, Dustin," I snapped, then I carefully leaned him against Detective Roland and walked over to the other side of the altar.

"What are you two talking about?" Roland demanded, not amused by our squabble.

"The reason my mom wants to put me in an asylum," I replied, spreading my hands out over the side of the altar. I'd never pushed the altar myself, considering I'd only been there once before and Dustin had been the one to push it, but I was sure I could do it even if I lacked the energy. "We can see ghosts."

Roland let out a snort of laughter. "Ghosts don't exist."

"Try telling that to the one in the room," Dustin mumbled as Jenny came floating in.

"Mimi, what are you doing?" she asked as she saw me readying myself to push the altar forwards. "You aren't seriously thinking about desecrating an altar, are you? Jeez, and to think that you're the holy one."

Roland jumped at the sound of Jenny's voice. "Who said that?!" he demanded, spinning around with his flashlight, sending Dustin off-balance and back to the floor.

I looked up with surprise. "Wait, you heard that?" My gaze shifted to Dustin. "You don't think—"

"No, I don't think very often, but when I do, it's with deep contemplation and reasoning," he replied, cutting me off before I could give us away.

Sighing, I repositioned and began to push on the altar. At first, nothing happened, then all at once, the altar gave and began to move forwards, revealing a dark stone staircase leading down into the unknown abyss.

"Just when I thought the night couldn't get any stranger," Roland exclaimed in amazement, stepping over to the edge of the altar and dragging Dustin with him.

Before he could take another step, I stopped him. "I need your oath; you will keep this place silent. You will not breathe a word of this place and what happens here to another soul, creature, inanimate object, or anything else as long as you live."

Roland looked at me, seeing the gravity in my features, and nodded. "You have my word."

"Great, now can you uncuff me? I'd rather not fall for the next fifteen minutes," Dustin said, holding up his wrist and Roland's.

"No, you're going down with me, chained just as you are," Roland replied firmly. "And there will be absolutely no funny business, are we clear?"

Dustin just glared.

I decided to descend the steps first. I took the first step and felt a rippling pain shoot through my veins. Something didn't want me to climb down the staircase. Ignoring the pain, I took another step, and it doubled. On the third, I doubled over and let out a scream.

Dustin dragged Roland down the steps to me. "Mimi, what's wrong?" he asked as my scream freaked him out.

"She cannot descend the steps," a voice from above answered.

I looked up and gasped. It was Charlie.

But it wasn't the Charlie I knew, the geeky one with the messy auburn hair and black rimmed glasses. This was a different one, the one I encountered two months ago, the one who threw the blades at me.

"Get out of the way," he commanded Roland and Dustin.

Dustin didn't want to budge, but Roland dragged him back up the steps just as Charlie jumped down to the ones below me.

I felt sick with pain, unable to move, unable to speak.

Charlie bent down and scooped me up into his arms, then placed me back onto the floor of the chapel above.

The pain stopped.

I gasped the air back into my lungs and stared at Charlie in disbelief. "How'd you—"

"Get here? Know—?"

"Lose the glasses?" Dustin cut in. "Yeah, we'd like to know all of that."

Charlie ignored Dustin's remark, but instead placed his eyes on Roland. "An adult, huh? Well, I hope he has as much faith as young people do, because we're going to need all the faith we can get if we're going to stop the demon who poisoned you, Mimi."

"Excuse me," Roland said, becoming annoyed that he didn't know what was going on. "But would you kindly explain who you are, and what you're talking about?"

"Isn't it obvious?" Dustin retorted, looking from Roland to me.

I gave him my blank stare.

He gave me his dumbfounded look. "Mimi, you seriously don't know?"

"Know what?"

"Jeez, you're the religious one, and I'm the one who knows." He shook his head then looked at Jenny. "And I bet you don't know either."

"Know what?" Jenny asked, causing Roland to look around again.

"Know the truth, Jenny," Charlie replied, looking straight at her.

"You can see me?" Jenny asked, surprised at this.

"And hear you, since the beginning," Charlie said with a nod.

"Why didn't you tell us?" I asked, still not grasping the concept.

"I couldn't tell you; you were never supposed to find out."

"Find out what?" Jenny demanded.

"That he's your Guardian Angel, Meems," Dustin answered, trying to cross his arms across his chest but only managing to cross one and half-cross the other as Roland yanked his arm back.

I stared at Dustin, then at Charlie. "You're an angel?" My mind felt like mush. Charlie was an angel, one sent from heaven.

"I thought angels were perfect," Jenny said, circling Charlie. "You told me to 'go to hell' once, if I recall."

"Only God is perfect," Charlie replied, keeping his eyes on Jenny. "Angels make mistakes too, it's a default of being created. Our emotions can become strong enough to cloud our sense of judgment, just like mortals, however, we answer straight to the Big Guy for all our sins and failures. I pray that you forgive me for that, Jennifer."

Jenny's lips curved into a smile. "Oh, I forgive you, I just—angel, my boyfriend is an angel. Does that mean—?" She stretched out her slim fingers and touched Charlie. No actually, she touched him. She pulled her hand back.

"I'm not fully here, but I'm not fully there, either. I'm a being of two realms, one of this world and the next, a being of many times and places. I can touch those who have moved on, along with those who haven't," he explained. "I'm really sorry, Jenny."

"It's okay, I—I'll try to understand." Her form flickered slightly, then she looked down the steps. "I'll be—downstairs . . . if you need me." And with that, she disappeared.

"Well, that sure put a rain on your relationship," Dustin summed up happily.

I glared at him. "You and I are going to have a one-on-one later, and you're not going to like it," I told him.

"Good luck with that," Dustin said holding up his arm that was cuffed to Detective Roland. "I think we'll have an eavesdropper."

"I can always cuff you to something that can't be moved, like a pillar," Roland said, smiling at the satisfaction that would bring him.

"Okay, let's go back to the main issue here," I said, bringing round the conversation. "Why can't I go down the steps?"

"Because your blood is tainted with the ungodly. If you try to enter anywhere that is completely sacred, it will burn you alive, just like it would do to the ungodly," Charlie explained.

"Then how come she could enter the cemetery?" Roland asked. We all stared at him, but he held his ground. "You say demons cannot enter holy grounds, then why could she if she has tainted blood?"

"Because she is one of ours," Charlie replied. "She is mortal, and mortals can cross the barriers that the angelic cannot. You must remember that demons were of the angels once, but they sided with Lucifer and fell, becoming misshapen creatures of the abyss. A demon cannot enter these grounds unless it is powerful enough to break in but can never enter any place that is sacred like my library. Only I can grant permission, and demons will never obtain it."

"I think I liked you better when you were pretending to be human," Dustin decided. "You didn't have this strange formality air going on."

"I can kick your butt if you'd like me to," Charlie told him, and I smiled. Angel or not, Charlie and Dustin were never going to get along.

"Do you know how to cure demonic poison?" I asked hopefully.

Charlie looked away. My heart sank; even the angels couldn't look me in the eyes. "Mimi, I've been searching through my entire library all week to find a way to break your con—" He stopped as if he were going to say something he'd regret.

"My connection with the demon?" I finished for him. "My soul is connected to the demon's, isn't it? When I die, it's going to steal my soul."

He didn't answer.

"ANSWER ME CHARLIE!" I yelled, feeling my heart freeze as if someone dunked it in liquid nitrogen.

"Yes."

"There's got to be a way to reverse it, right?" Dustin asked, becoming just as anxious as me. "Someone must have been poisoned by a demon before and was cured, right? It's not like it has power over her or anything with this connection."

"Oh, the fallen have power over their victims," Charlie replied truthfully.

"Great, so if I would have died last week, my soul had a chance at redemption," I stated, throwing my hands up in the air. "Wonderful, just wonderful!

"Don't give up yet, Mimi, we still have time to find a solution," Charlie said, looking down the steps. "Have faith, put your trust in God, and we will find a way."

"If God cared, he wouldn't have let this happen to her in the first place," Dustin replied, gesturing to me.

"Dustin," I warned, but he didn't listen.

"No, it is true, and his angel can attest to it. If God truly cared about people, he wouldn't let them suffer and fight their demons on their own. He would help fight!"

Charlie clenched his fists, and I held my breath. If those two started fighting now, I doubted either one of them would turn out all right, hell, I wouldn't turn out alright. They were wasting the precious little time I had left. "Suffering is caused by man, not by God. Remember that, Harper," he said dangerously, and then he descended the steps and disappeared into the darkness.

"Well, that went better than I thought it would," Dustin said when he could no longer see Charlie.

I glared at him, then turned to Detective Roland. "It takes about fifteen minutes to reach the bottom. Down there is a work that will tell us how to defeat the demon and get your partner back. I suggest you help Charlie find it."

Roland didn't say anything, but instead, he began to lead Dustin down the steps.

"Mimi," Dustin tried to protest.

"Go, help them, Dustin." I turned and went towards the door. "I'll be fine up here."

Roland pushed him down the steps before he could try and protest again. I waited until they were completely down the steps before I walked out the door. The air was colder than it had been before, the wind dropping the temp to hover just above forty degrees. I pulled the windbreaker tighter around my shoulders and sat down on the steps.

My life seemed to have plummeted over the course of the past few days. Not only had I lost the trust for my mother, the safety of my own roof, and the strength of my own body, but I also was losing the one thing I valued the most; my own soul. If I'd died in that alley last week, if my soul had risen out of my body then, maybe I would have escaped the fate that awaited me in the coming days. Maybe then I wouldn't be the calling card for one of the forsaken. Fate's cruel like that.

I leaned down and picked up a stone from the path, then I held it in my hand. I felt the sharp edges and the smooth facets as I turned the stone in my hand. There had to be more to the end than this, more of a fight. What hero survives the trials just to be cut down in the end?

You're not a hero, though, Matilda.

I chucked the stone at the ground and stood up. It's true, I'm not a hero, nor have I ever been one. I was just some kid who got caught up in the middle of some sort of supernatural struggle; just another casualty in the war of worlds. All I had batting for me was a delinquent, a ghost, an angel, and partially a cop, err excuse me, a detective. I think I preferred life better when I thought I was just going to die.

I could just kill myself.

That could work, I mean, at least then I had a chance at escaping the demon before it could reach me.

I discarded that idea. If I killed myself, that would earn me an eternity in hell. Suicide is a sin, right up there with murder. Taking a life before the time God decides, even if it's your own life, is breaking one of the commandments.

So, I was stuck.

My knees began to buckle, and I sank back down onto the cold stone steps of the chapel. When you hit bottom, you hit it hard. The acceleration downwards causes enough force to completely shatter everything you have in you; all the muscles, bones, tissues, strength, self-confidence, even your faith. At the bottom of the hole lies all that you were; along with broken dreams and memories of everything at the top, everything that happened on the way down is right there with you too. It's said that hitting rock bottom is good, that when you hit it, there's only one direction to go, and that's up.

What they don't mention is this: you don't have to go up.

I put my head in my hands and began to cry silently. No one was around to hear me, no one but the dead who wander the desolate graves by the light of the crescent moon, the ones who are so far gone that they take no notice to passersby, or even to those who can see them. Yet even though no one could hear me, I kept silent.

I probably sat there crying for a few hours, feeling my life slip by, slowly trickling down the drain into the eternity of hell that awaited me sooner rather than later. The only sound that came as comfort were the growing crashes from the storm brewing in the distance. When I was little, my parents told me that the sound of thunder was the angels bowling up in heaven, and that the lightning came from the celebration of getting strikes. I remembered that as I sat there, waiting for fate to take hold.

"*Matilda,*" the call came from the edge of my consciousness. It was so silent that I wasn't sure that I had heard it at all. Then it continued in a slow rhythmic chant, calling me, beckoning me to follow it, to listen to it. My heart rate began to climb as fear gripped my heart; whatever was happening, it couldn't be good.

"*Angel of God, my guardian dear—*" I began to pray aloud.

"*Matilda Josephine Blake.*"

The words faltered on my tongue, and I fell victim to the chant. Nothing mattered anymore except the soft beat and keeping to the soft rhythmic beat. All the pain and suffering melted away like ice off the side of the hill in mid spring. My fear vanished as well, vanquished by the rhythm.

"*Push the altar back, and tie the door shut,*" the rhythm demanded.

Immediately, I complied. Walking into the chapel, I headed towards the altar and pushed it back over the steps, blocking the only way out. I heard voices coming from beneath it, but they seemed distant and far off as if they belonged in a different world. I began to frown, but the rhythm told me not to worry, that as long as I cooperated, it would be fine.

My feet moved on their own as I walked out to Dustin's car and removed the rope he kept in the trunk in case his car went into the ditch. Taking the rope, I returned to the front of the chapel and closed the doors, tying the handles shut, and smiled.

"*Come join me, Matilda,*" the rhythm beckoned. "*Join me, and all your worries will melt away.*"

No, stop! The intuitive side of me fought against the beat. *This is some kind of hypnosis, you're in danger! This is causing you to fall into a trance; you have to beat it!*

"*Matilda Josephine Blake; come out and play,*" the rhythm beckoned once again, and the last bit of control I had was blotted out.

Before I realized I was moving, my feet had carried me halfway across the cemetery and towards the center gate.

CHAPTER TWELVE:

I just about touched the metal of the center gate when someone grabbed me from behind.

"M, are you alright?" It was Teddy. He looked ruffled; his hair was mishap and disheveled, as if he'd just rolled out of bed, and his clothes were tattered and dirty, as if he'd just completed the Mud Man Five K run. What was he doing in the cemetery this late at night looking like that?

Wait a second, what was I doing?

"M, are you okay?" Teddy repeated, the pitch rising with each word. Thunder rolled in the distance, giving the air an electric feel. The storm was coming.

"No, and don't touch me!" I replied, yanking my arm out of his grip, still trying to shake my nerves loose. The chanting had stopped playing like the speakers suddenly broke, and my brain was working double time to make up for the loss of control. "What are you doing here, Theodore?"

He stared at me, then replied, "I just ran here after being chased by this creature that jumped me while I was filling my tank. I hardly made it here alive. See these cuts, they're from that thing's talons." He lifted his shirt, revealing slash marks across his chest and abdomen. Those were definitely not from any wolf I'd seen; they were from something far more sinister.

"Why come here to the cemetery?" I asked.

"Because that's the closest place with a building. It destroyed the station just up the road, you can even see the flames on the horizon." Teddy turned me and pointed at a distant spot just over the fence that was glowing orange. "M, we've got to get out of here."

I shook him off once again and glared at him. "I'm not going anywhere with you. Not after all you've put me through!"

"What? Why do you—?"

"No! You have no right! You toyed with me and now you expect me to—"

"*Matilda Josephine Blake,*" the rhythm started up again, and I lost control just as before.

"M?" Teddy asked, horrified as my face went blank.

"*Come out and play.*"

I took a step towards the gate, but Teddy grabbed me and began to drag me away as I kicked and fought. "M! Listen to me! The monster is trying to get you! You have to ignore it, fight!" His voice was filled with horror.

"LET ME GO!" I screamed at him, clawing and kicking as much as I could. The voice wanted me to go to the gate, and he was taking me away. I had to listen to the voice!

"No, I won't let you go, not this time." He held onto me tighter, dragging me back down the path towards the chapel.

"ACK! HELP ME! I'M GETTING KIDNAPPED!" I screamed into the air, saying anything I could to get him to release me. The further he dragged me, the worse the desire to reach the gate became until it suddenly just broke.

The voice was gone once again.

I stopped fighting Teddy and began to tremble.

"M?" he asked, no longer dragging me.

"Teddy," I said, my voice shaking, "you have to let me go."

He snorted. "M, I know I'm not a very good guy, but that thing—it's not safe. It'll tear you to pieces if it were to get close enough! It nearly killed me!"

"That's because it's not you it wants, it's me, and it won't harm me."

"You don't know that, M," Teddy insisted as he dragged me towards the front steps of the chapel.

"I do know that, Theodore, because it's here to take my soul."

Teddy released his hold on my arm and stared at me.

"When you told me about that ghost stuff, you weren't joking."

I shook my head. "No, I was telling you the truth."

Teddy stared at me and an expression of guilt and understanding overcame his features. "I thought you were taking a turn down crazy street, M."

"I know."

"You didn't stop me."

"I know."

"I was only trying to protect you."

I bit my lip. "I almost killed myself that day," I admitted, turning away so he couldn't see my tears. "You were the only thing in my life I had left, and you broke me the day I lost everything!" I burst into tears again.

"I'm so sorry, M, I thought I was doing you a favor," he replied, attempting to put his arm around me.

There was no way I was going to let him string me along like that again. "Well, you thought wrong, didn't you?!" I threw a punch at him and hit him square in the jaw. "That's for all the pain you caused me!"

He put his hand on the other side of his jaw and popped it back into place. "I deserved that," he admitted.

"And this," I threw another punch and hit him on the other side of the jaw, "is for two-timing with Trisha!" The tears streamed down my face, but the punches felt good. All the pent-up anger I'd been biting down for the past few months had finally been expelled by a few good roundhouses to the jaw. At least when I joined the damned in hell, that wouldn't be on my chest.

He spat out some blood and wiped the rest from his split lip, then stared at me as if he hadn't deserved the second punch. "I wasn't dating Trisha back then."

My anger flared. "You're a liar! Jenny told me she saw you kissing her in the hallway a few days before she died!" I got ready to punch him again.

"She kissed me!" Teddy protested. "Jenny missed the part when I threw her off!"

"Well you missed the part when dating someone you made out with when you already had a girlfriend that you broke up with because you met a new girl is wrong and two-timing!" I yelled at him.

"M, I only went out with Trisha because I wanted to make you jealous."

I let out a maniacal laugh. This was just too much for me to hear. "Jealous? How can you be jealous of me?"

Teddy became angry as well. "Hmm, let's see. How about your new boyfriend, the one who you spend all your time with? What's his name . . . oh right, Dustin Harper!"

I stared at him. "I'm not dating Dustin!"

"What?" Teddy asked as he took a step back in surprise.

"Yeah, we aren't dating! We're just friends."

"Huh." Teddy raised his hand to his head awkwardly trying to brush off his humiliation. "So, I dated crazy Trish for nothing."

"Hold on, dated crazy Trish, as in, you're no longer dating?" I asked, my mind becoming more boggled with each passing second.

"Yeah, I broke up with her the day after you got in the fight. I was going to tell you that when we were in the café, the day you . . . ."

"Oh," I said, not sure where this conversation was headed. "Well, I—um, this is awkward."

"Yep."

I stared at him, trying to allow myself to believe him, to let things go back to the way they were. I wanted to, it would have been so easy to just accept everything he said, to believe he still wanted me because he loved me. To have him be my everything once again.

"Let's get out of here now, Matilda, before that thing reaches us." He held out his hand for me to take.

But I knew better.

I swatted his hand away. "No. I won't fall for you again." Then, I walked around him and began walking back towards the chapel to release my friends.

"M! What the hell?" he demanded, running so that he could block me. "I thought I got through to you."

I glared at him. "Get out of my way."

"No, we are getting out of here," he replied strictly, grabbing my arm.

"Let go of my arm, Theodore," I growled, trying to pull my arm from his grasp once again.

His grip only became tighter. "No. You will listen to me. Or do I have to remind you who makes the decisions?"

I could feel my blood vessels breaking under his hand as his grip became unbearably tight. "I make my own decisions, and you're not one of them."

"You don't have the strength."

I kicked him in the balls, and he doubled over, releasing my arm, revealing the newly forming bruise in the shape of his hand. "You know, I was lying when I said Dustin was just a friend. He's more a man than you'll ever be."

Teddy looked up at me and laughed, still in pain. "You think he cares about you? No one could ever care about you! He'll use you, just like everyone else in your past has. He'll leave you, just like Jenny left you. You'll see, M, when he cuts you to pieces, and you'll regret not choosing me."

"We'll see about tha—AHHHH!" I let out a scream and toppled over as my blood began to boil.

I began to writhe with pain, unspeakable and unbearable pain. Someone must have lit a match in my veins because they were on fire, burning with the intensity of the same caliber as when I was in the alley.

"MATILDA!" A voice came from over by the chapel. "MATILDA! WHERE ARE YOU?!" It was Dustin's.

My heart leapt; they had managed to get out after all.

There was a loud crashing sound at the center gate of the cemetery, and a dark creature the size of a small Toyoda stumbled in. It was black, a creature created from the dark abyss, and monstrous. It looked slightly humanoid. However, the foot-long talons on the end of each of its six fingers begged to differ. It stalked into the cemetery, its yellow eyes searching for its prey, and falling upon Teddy, it began to move rapidly towards us.

The storm was finally upon us.

CHAPTER THIRTEEN:

Teddy did nothing but stare stupidly at the monster that had just broke the sacred barrier of the cemetery.

Never before had I seen a creature of the abyss, and never do I ever want to see one again. As a kid, my father told me that no evil creature could break the holy barriers that surrounded sacred places like churches and cemeteries. An invisible force fields exist that keep them out. I'd seen them before; capturing the demon in a circle of salt was one such case of invisible force fields, but this, this was horrifying. This monster was stronger than anything I'd ever faced; that most Mortuus Loquis had ever faced.

However, when it broke the barrier, the pain stopped, leaving me exhausted and nearly unconscious. This creature must've had a tie to the demon, or, more terrifying yet, it was the demon, and it was drawing its power from me.

Oh God, I was the lifeline to the demon! Wait, did that mean that if we vanquished the demon, it would also vanquish me? Bad, bad, bad, not good, oh horrible, horrible, terrible, horrifying, tiring! Draining. I was tired; maybe a quick nap would fix things. No, now was not the time for a nap! Now was the time for a fight!

I prayed that the boys had come across some kind of cure, a way to break my connection with the demon.

The doors to the chapel flew open, revealing the angelic Charlie and his sword of angels. Light radiated off him like a beacon of hope. It burned my eyes, so I looked away. Go figure that out of the two of us, I was the one becoming a forsaken and Dustin was the one fighting with the angels. Oh, the irony.

Teddy froze when he saw Charlie standing majestically within the door frame of the chapel. He looked at me, then back at Charlie, and let out a low mumble, "What the hell is going on with the world?"

"Charlie's an angel, by the way," I groaned, trying to keep my eyes off Charlie.

"Right, of course he is, because angels are completely normal." Teddy shook his head, then looked back at the monster. It had covered more than half the distance to the chapel, and it would be only a matter of seconds before it was right on top of us.

"Get her in the chapel!" Charlie commanded Teddy as he stepped down the stone steps, his sword held in a fighting position.

Teddy reached down and picked me up, against my protest, and dove past Charlie and into the chapel, tripping over the last step. Of course, that sent me flying into the granite altar.

I moaned in pain as Dustin came to my side. He was no longer cuffed to Detective Roland, so I figured that Roland had come over to our side. All the better for us, the other side didn't have cookies. "Mimi, I got you," he said, pulling me into his arms. "Everything is going to be okay; I've got you."

"Get your hands off my girlfriend!" Teddy growled, pushing himself back to his feet.

Dustin looked at him, then to me. "You've got to be kidding me, Meems."

"I'm not your girlfriend!" I moaned.

Roland stepped between us and Teddy. "That's enough, kid. Leave the girl alone."

Dustin stuck his tongue out at Teddy, just to prove that he won this round, then held me closer to his chest.

"What is that thing?!" Roland asked when he saw the creature outside approaching Charlie from over Teddy's shoulder.

"The demon," I croaked, trying to keep from passing out.

"No . . . it can't be . . . the barrier," Dustin said, his brain not processing the data.

"It broke the barrier using my strength. It's drawing its power from me, Dustin, I can't stop it." My head fell against his chest as my eyelids began to droop.

"Mimi, you stay with me, now. Don't you dare close your eyes!" Dustin cried, putting my head in his hands. "Don't give up on me now!"

"Did you find a way to stop it?" I asked, trying to comply with his orders.

"We found out what it is. But I'm not sure why it's here," Dustin lied, trying to keep me calm.

"BE GONE, DEMON!" Charlie bellowed at the creature that stood only a few feet away. "BE GONE OR TASTE THE LIGHT OF GOD!"

The creature let out a blood curdling maniacal laugh, similar to the one I had earlier. "Ah, Charlemagne the Immortal Protector, how little your threat means to me," the demon replied. "You fight the battle that will destroy you."

Charlie stood his ground. "You are one of the forsaken now; you have no right to be here!"

"I have every right, just as you, to do as I please." It took a step forwards, and Charlie swung at it with his sword, cutting its leg and spilling black ooze onto the grass, causing it to wither and die. It let out an angry cry, swiping its talons at Charlie's throat, but Charlie parried the attack with his sword and sidestepped the second pair.

"You have no right!" Charlie persisted, awaiting the next attack from the creature. "You lost that right the day you chose to follow he who fell. You are nothing but a traitorous monster." Charlie spat on the ground.

"Just give up the girl, Charlemagne, she belongs to me now. You can see her there, she's just about gone. Why do you protect one who will die shortly anyways?"

"I won't damn her, nor any other soul. Today, the only soul going to hell will be yours!"

"I gave you the chance, but you did not comply. Now her soul, and the soul of the rest of those whom you protect, shall be mine!" The demon charged in, sending Charlie into full battle mode.

"Screw you demon! It never even told me what I wasn't supposed to do." I mumbled angrily. I'd gone through hell because of this thing, and it never even told me why.

Wait a second.

What was the one thing that had carried through this entire adventure? The one thing that kept showing up?

"The locket!" I said, trying to reach up and pull the thing from my neck. "Dustin, the locket!"

"What about it?" Dustin demanded.

"That's what it wants; that's the thing it's after!" It made perfect sense! The demon had shown me a locket just like this one when I was dying in the alley, and the demon didn't start coming after me until I was in possession of it. It was a lot easier to believe than it wanting to haunt Dustin! The demon wanted the locket, and it wanted it badly.

Dustin jumped on the bandwagon, and he tore the locket from my neck and held it in his hand. "I'll make sure it gets it, Mimi, you stay right there."

I grabbed his arm. "Dustin, don't! That thing is no longer just after the locket, it wants us all dead!"

He leaned down and kissed me on the lips. "Matilda, don't do anything stupid until I get back."

I clung to his arm. "Dustin, please, you can hardly walk! It'll kill you!"

"Mimi, it's the only way. I have to lead it away from you, I have to keep you safe."

"Then let me do it," Teddy said, standing up to walk over to us.

Dustin raised his brow. "You want to do this, Dolly?"

"Teddy," Teddy replied coldly, "and yes, I do. I see how it's supposed to be now, how I can atone for my sins."

I stared at him in confusion; his words–they didn't sound like him. It was as if someone had put the words in his mouth.

Dustin stared him in the eyes for a couple seconds, then nodded his head, and I watched as he handed the locket over to Teddy.

"Dustin, what are you doing?!" I cried. "He's not–"

"I already know that, Mimi," Dustin replied softly.

"But–"

"I realized when I saw that thing that I wasn't going to make it through the night," Teddy cut me off, holding up the locket "but I won't let anyone else die because I didn't do the right thing. Not today, at least." He gave me a tough smile. "Besides, God's giving me a chance to make it right for you. Second chances don't come without a price."

"But this isn't you making the decision! You don't believe in God."

"There's a lot of things I didn't believe a few hours ago." Teddy looked out the doors of the chapel at Charlie. "Turns out, they were true."

"Nobody has to die tonight, not even you, no matter how much you might deserve it," I pleaded, trying to break through to him. I know he did a lot of horrible things, especially to me, but he wasn't making this decision. He didn't make this kind of decision. Nobody should have to have choices made for them, no matter how bad they are. It was as if–no, why would he? He's an angel.

Dustin pulled me into his arms and held me tightly so I wouldn't do anything stupid. "Let him do it Meems."

"No! This isn't right. Teddy, this isn't you! Why am I the only one who sees this?"

"Guard her with your life, you hear me?" Teddy commanded Dustin.

"I hear you," Dustin said with a nod. "I won't let you down, Ted."

"Stop talking about me as if I'm not here!" I cried angrily. God, boys are such a-holes.

Teddy gave me one last wink, then turned to face the spectacle outside. The clouds gave out with a thunderous crash as the rain began falling in heavy sheets onto the ground, making it near impossible to see anything. I could still hear the battle raging on outside as Charlie and the demon continued to fight.

I closed my eyes and began to pray for Charlie as the demon continued raging battle against him. Even though Charlie was an angel, I didn't see him as one. I saw him as my best friend, fighting for the sake of his best friend, his worst enemy, and some cop he didn't even know. Charlie was a true hero, in all senses of the word.

The battle escalated, and suddenly, Charlie got thrown through the open doors of the chapel and up against the far back wall. He crumbled down behind the altar just as another flash of lightning lit up the darkened ash skies. The silhouette of the black creature appeared in the doorway as another crash of thunder and lightning sounded.

My heart pounded; this was the end.

Charlie crawled out from behind the altar, his sword still clutched tightly in his hand. His hair was matted in his own blood and he held his left arm close to his chest, mangled and bending in places that no arm should bend. Water dripped from his soaked skin, creating a puddle everywhere he went. He made eye contact with me and I read what was scrawled across them loud and clear: *I'm sorry.*

He couldn't defeat the demon; he could only prolong our deaths.

No, this couldn't be the end, we couldn't all just die, not after all we'd been through! Anger and outrage swelled up in my chest, and I pushed past my tired limbs and stood. "Charlie, I need your sword."

He shook his head. "No, I can't give it to you. The light might kill you at this point."

"Charlie, we have no other choice. If I don't do this now, then we're all going to die for sure. We have to give it one last go."

"Mimi, I'm your Guardian Angel, I'll protect you until my dying breath. I won't let you stand up to that creature on your own," Charlie said firmly.

"I won't be alone," I replied grimly. "I have you, Dustin, Jenny, Teddy, and Detective Roland to back me up. I have to try."

Charlie stared at the stone floor, debating my words. "I wish I could keep you out of this fight, just like I told Jenny," he said grimly.

"Charlie please."

"Mimi," Dustin said anxiously. "It'll kill you."

"Then I might as well give it what it wants," I said with grim resolve. It was time that I fought my own demons.

Charlie saw the resolve in my face; he understood that I wasn't going to back down and reached a decision. Raising the sword, he told me "God's speed," and presented me with it.

I nodded, then I reached out and grabbed the sword.

What I expected was to ripple in pain due to the demonic energies that were in me. What I didn't expect was to feel—good? Is that how you explain holy power? You'd think it would be a strong wave of strength surging through your veins, but it's nothing like that. In reality, it's like a soft wind that comes and surrounds you with the warm comfort that you're not alone. It's calming and a great confidence boost.

Looking down at the sword in my hand, I saw, for the first time, the realities of what the poison was doing to me. The light from the sword brought out the blackness of the poison in my veins; all the way up my arm, my veins were black. I shuddered to think how much more was like that.

I faced the demon, holding the sword tightly in both hands. "This ends tonight," I said, holding the sword up high enough to signal that I was going to fight. Teddy was standing on my left-hand side, and Detective Roland was at my right, his gun drawn and ready to shoot. "You can have the locket, then leave in peace, or we're going to banish you; the choice is yours."

A cold rumble came from its lips and I figured that meant it was going for option three which was to completely annihilate us. This demon was out to raze, and it was going to bring hell with it.

"Alright, the latter it is!" I yelled and charged the demon.

I guess now's as good a time as ever to inform you about my lack of coordination with external objects not connected to my body. Putting it simply: I have no proprioception.

Drawing the sword back, I aimed to level a blow at its side, hoping to give it a fatal wound and end the battle right then.

What actually happened: drawing the sword back, I charged the demon. It sidestepped me easily, causing me to tumble down the front steps of the chapel face-first into the mud.

Woops.

The demon stalked its way towards me, laughing maniacally. I guess my sad attempt at heroism really was that pitiful.

Still clutching the sword, I swiped at it, pushing myself backwards, crawling on my back, away from the demon. It easily parried my attack, cooing slightly, taunting me.

"Poor Matilda Blake," it cooed. "She only wanted to protect the ones she loved, but through that want to protect, she brought about their deaths. Do you now see the frailty of light? How darkness swallows it whole?"

I crawled back into the monument which stood sentry over the peaceful souls. There was no more room to retreat.

This was the end.

I held the sword as tightly as I could, the fear rippling through me as the rain continued to fall in sheets from the sky. My tears were masked by the immense amount of water as I stared into the eyes of death.

"Ah, you fear the end. You fear that I will kill you now, put an end to you before the others." It stretched out a talon and put it under my chin, forcing me to raise my head.

I closed my eyes as the tears slipped out more profusely than before and awaited my death.

But the demon had something else in mind, something far worse than my death.

"*Matilda Josephine Blake,*" it said, pronouncing each syllable perfectly. "*Retrieve the locket from your friends, then kill them, slowly and painfully.*"

The voice in the back of my mind didn't even sound this time; the demon had completed its control over me and there was nothing I could do about it.

I stood, lifting the sword with me, and walked slowly towards the chapel.

"MATILDA STOP!" Jenny's voice came from the back of my conscious, but it had no effect. I kept walking.

"M?" Teddy's voice quavered as I walked towards him and the locket that dangled in his grasps.

"Teddy, that's no longer Mimi," Charlie said, crawling to the door of the chapel as Roland ran out to stand between me and Teddy in the pouring rain. "Mimi's gone. The demon has her, and we can't reach her any longer. You have to kill her." He closed his eyes and the tears escaped.

Roland and Teddy backed away from the chapel as I continued at the slow pace, unable to make the connection of what they were saying to me. The words were there in my head, but they didn't seem to register.

"There must be a way to bring her back!" Dustin begged Charlie, but he shook his head.

"I'm sorry Dustin. I've seen many good people become lost due to this, and there is no way for us to stop it."

"That's not good enough!" Teddy agreed with Dustin, planting his feet.

"Kill her, Roland, kill her or she'll kill us all," Charlie commanded him.

Roland aimed his Glock at me. "Come on, kid, don't make me kill you."

I continued to approach, my face blank like my mind. The fear and pleading didn't mean anything to me, neither did my own life.

"*Matilda Josephine Blake!*" Jenny appeared at the doors to the chapel as I felt the control from the demon begin to weaken. "*Matilda Josephine Blake!*" She floated out and towards me, in order to move the line of fire from the boys to me.

"What are you doing?" the demon demanded angrily, trying to advert her change in command over me.

"I'm stopping you from winning, you dirty slime-bag," Jenny threw back at it in pure defiance. "*Matilda Josephine Blake! I command you to stop!*"

It was as if the glass bubble in which my free will watched in apathy shattered and a flood of emotion and horror flowed back into my mind. I let out a piercing scream as it did and dropped the sword. It clattered into the mud, leaving me completely defenseless. I curled up into a ball and cried as Roland lowered his gun and moved out of sight.

Teddy ran to my side as the demon let out an angry cry and attacked Jenny.

"You insolent little spirit!" it bellowed, no longer able to control its anger and frustration. Jenny had managed to destroy the entirety of its plan in less than two minutes. I almost felt sorry for it; she'd done the same to me many times, and I could sympathize with how annoying that was. "I should have captured your soul the day I destroyed your body."

Jenny floated towards it with her hands on her hips. Her blonde hair remained dry since the rain flowed through her, creating an unreal sensation as I stared at her while she stood up to the creature that killed her. "You may have destroyed my body, and you may take my soul, but I will not let you take her soul. The only one who can mess with Matilda is me, ya big ugly blob."

It screeched and took out the locket it had shown me in the alley last week.

"JENNY LOOK OUT!" I screamed, but it was too late.

The demon swung the locket out, capturing her in it, her soul now gone forever.

"JENNY!" I screamed, drawing the attention back onto me. This couldn't be happening, she couldn't be gone, not after everything. She couldn't be gone. It just couldn't be possible.

Slowly, the demon turned its gaze back towards me and I could see the victory in its yellow eyes. It'd succeeded in taking my greatest ally and friend, the one who saved me, the one protecting me since the beginning. It'd already defeated each and every one of us, and now as it stepped towards me, it remained silent. The demon no longer needed words to horrify me.

BANG! BANG! BANG! The sound of gunshots rang through the night; the frequency strong enough to break your teeth. Roland fired three rounds through the demon's chest, which should have been enough to kill it.

The demon let out an angry cry and turned on Roland. "Your partner would be ashamed of your performance,

Demetrius Roland," the demon taunted, changing tactics. "He assured me there was more fight in you. Well, you can join him in hell now, Detective." The demon lunged at Roland, who dove out of the way just in time. The demon crashed into the graves, breaking some and mangling others as more of the acidic goo dripped from its wounds.

I had to get up, I had to rejoin the fight. Reaching for the sword, I rolled over and found it gone, somehow managing to vanish within the few seconds that my eyes had left it. "Ah crud," I swore, trying to spot it in the nonexistent lighting. It shouldn't be that hard to find a glowing sword in the dark.

"Mimi," a voice in the dark startled me as a hand grabbed my arm and wrenched me to my feet. "Mimi, we've got to get to cover." Dustin stumbled slightly under my weight, but we had enough strength between the two of us to remain standing.

"I've got to find the sword!" I protested, not wanting it to fall into the hands of the demon.

"HEY!" yelled Teddy, his figure illuminated by the light of the glowing sword in his hand. I hadn't even noticed that he'd left my side. He stood just behind the demon and slashed it with the sword before it could charge Roland again. "YOU WANT THE LOCKET?! COME AND GET IT, YOU OVERSIZED SHADOW PUPPET!"

So much for finding the sword and keeping it from the demon.

"Teddy no!" I screamed, but it was too late. The demon lunged at Teddy and sliced off the hand holding the locket in one fluid movement, and it toppled to the ground. Teddy shrieked in pain, and before he could react, the demon sent three talons through his abdomen. Blood bubbled out of his lips as the light left his shocked eyes.

"NOOO!" I screamed, attempting to run towards him, but Dustin held me back. "NO! LET ME GO! TEDDY!"

"He's gone, Meems. He's gone and we're about to follow."

CHAPTER FOURTEEN:

I shook as I watched the demon slowly rip Teddy to shreds, demonstrating how it was going to do the same to us. This was wrong, it was all so wrong! Nobody was supposed to die like this, the demon wasn't supposed to have the upper hand!

"This is wrong," I whispered.

"I know," Dustin replied, pulling me in close so that he could hold me one last time before we met our maker.

"No, I mean that the monsters aren't supposed to win."

"Well, try telling that to the one that's winning," Dustin remarked, pulling me back under the shelter of the chapel. Charlie and Detective Roland had both slipped back behind the doors and were now trying to come up with the end game in modest hopes that we could still win. Dustin sat me down behind the altar that had been pushed back to its original position and crouched down, glancing over the altar to check and see how much time we had remaining before the demon moved on to us.

"I say it can screw itself," I swore, reaching back for my bag.

Dustin saw what I was doing and handed it to me. "Mimi, there isn't anything in there that you haven't already tried," he told me. "You're grasping at straws."

"I will NOT sit tightly and watch as someone I care about gets filleted by a demon planning to do the same to me!" I screamed at him, digging for something, anything, that I could still use. I pulled out a pocket-knife, what remained of my holy water, chalk, a rosary, a bible, and the medal of Saint Benedict.

The medal of Saint Benedict—there was something about it that was special that I should remember. Oh, what was the story I heard that one Sunday at Sunday school?

"Come on! Think, Matilda; what is so special about the medal of Saint Benedict?"

"You have a Saint Benedict medal?" Charlie asked, crawling over, cradling his arm close to his chest.

"Yes, she does; what's so important about that?" Dustin demanded.

"There's supposedly an exorcism on the medal. When activated, it can cast away demons, or so the legend says," Detective Roland replied, joining us.

"You're telling me that we've had a way to exorcise this demon for the past—how long have you had that medal?!" Dustin exploded, his anger outweighing his shock, "And none of you had the decency to even mention this before?"

"I forgot I carried one on me," I replied defensively, pulling the medal closer to my chest in order to shield it from the wrath of Dustin.

"Jesus Christ," Dustin shook his head as Charlie gave him a deadly glare.

"I apologize for his words," Charlie told the sky above.

"Don't go apologizing for me!" Dustin told Charlie. "I don't go around apologizing for every God damn sin you've ever committed!"

"BOYS!" I yelled, "Now is not the time!" I handed the medal over to Charlie. "Can you use the exorcism inscribed in this medal to banish the demon?"

Charlie held the medal and frowned. "It isn't activated yet; I need to activate it before I can use it."

"How're you supposed to activate it?" Roland asked.

"The bible, just hand it to me, it'll only take me a few minutes," Charlie explained.

"We don't have minutes," I said, placing the bible in Charlie's uninjured hand.

"Then keep it occupied until I can activate it," Charlie said and began chanting in Latin.

The demon was finishing up with Teddy outside as it overheard Charlie chanting. It lifted a bloody talon and pointed at him. "You're next," it hissed, then quickly finished off gutting Teddy.

I quickly dug through my sack and found what remained of the salt. If we were going to stand a chance, we were going to need a barrier, even if it would kill me. I began to pour the salt around us, forming a circle and closing it with the last strength I had.

At least the demon wouldn't have much power to break it with.

Dustin took the pocketknife and dumped what remained of the holy water on it, clutching it tightly in his fist. "Well, at least we'll go down fighting now."

I tried to smile but I was too exhausted; my body felt like one of those gel pictures you stick to your window for decoration. So, I just laid there, hoping I wouldn't be needed.

Roland picked up the chalk and examined it. "What good is chalk supposed to do us?"

"Well, if you really want to know, salt isn't the only thing you can use to make a circle," Dustin scowled, picking up the rosary. "Salt can only go so far." He placed the rosary around my neck.

Roland nodded his head, then jumped out of the circle.

"Are you crazy?" Dustin demanded. "You got a death wish?"

Roland quickly formed a circle around him, holding his gun in his hand. "I am an officer of the law; it is my duty to protect you with my life."

"A lot of good that'll do us if you're dead," Dustin replied.

"Kid, just back me up." Roland took aim and shot the demon in the arm.

Dustin jumped to his feet as the demon charged at Roland, who stood his ground. Jumping out of the circle, Dustin rolled past the demon and out into the rain. He grabbed the sword and threw the pocketknife at the demon, hitting it square in the back.

Steam and agonized screams came from the demon as it tried to wrench the blade from its back. It turned to face Dustin, giving him a look of complete animosity. "I was going to save you for last, Mortuus Loquis, but now, I might as well kill you next."

Charlie finished chanting and his mind resurfaced to the present situation. "You've got to be kidding me. Now Dustin is in possession of my sword?!"

"Is that a . . . problem?" I asked, barely able to make the words audible.

"Yeah, I don't like it when he plays with my toys," Charlie replied childishly.

I mentally rolled my eyes and imagined myself smacking him over the back of the head as hard as I could. Angel or not, he still deserved it.

"Roland!" Charlie yelled. "Distract the demon so it takes its attention off of Dustin; we don't need another body on our heads."

"Roger!" Roland fired the last rounds in his gun and sent them into the back of the demon.

The demon screamed in annoyance and returned to attack Roland.

"YAAAHHH!" Dustin threw the sword, and it hit the demon square between the shoulder blades, causing it to fall to its knees.

Roland jumped out of his circle and quickly drew one around the demon as Charlie stood up and began reciting the Latin phrase on the back of the medal. "*Crux Sacra Sit Mihi Lux, Non Draco Sit Mihi Dux. Vade Retro, Satana! Nunquam Suade Mihi Vana. Sunt Mala Quae Libas Ipse Venena Bibas.*"

A huge pillar of light penetrated through the ceiling of the chapel and hit down on the demon. The demon shrieked and, in an instant, started dissolving into millions of smoldering pieces of ash that disintegrated into nothingness as they hit the ground. The only traces which remained as evidence of its existence were a few bullets, a pocketknife, the locket, and Charlie's sword in the center of the circle.

It was over; the demon vanquished.

CHAPTER FIFTEEN:

I was seized by a fit of pain an instant later. In a split second, Charlie was at my side, trying to hold me still so he could stop the pain.

Dustin came running in, drenched by the rain that was still falling hard. Thunder rolled and lightning flashed, and I felt the last of my strength slip out of my grasp.

"Her veins, they're black," Dustin observed as he touched my skin. His touch was hot, and I screamed when he touched me, like he was burning me with a searing hot piece of metal.

"It's the poison," Charlie said, trying to hold me still. "She's at the final stage."

"I thought you said we still had another day before it got this bad!" Dustin cried.

"She did, but that was before she decided to be a hero," Charlie snapped.

I wanted to yell at them to quit arguing, but I could only manage more tortured shrieks.

Detective Roland ran over and took the medal from Charlie. "The medal of Saint Benedict has more than one use, my friend," he told Charlie, placing it upon my chest. "Not only can it cast out demons, but it can also cure poison. Benedict is the patron saint of poisons."

The power in the medal began to flow through me like an antidote pulsing through my veins.

I vomited, covering the granite floor in black venom. It began eating away at the granite before it fizzled and disappeared completely.

Slowly, the pain subsided, and I could breathe again, no longer in agony but still extremely exhausted.

Dustin looked up at Roland. "How do you know so much about this stuff, Demetrius?" he demanded.

Roland glared at Dustin, not for the question, but because of the way he said his name. I guess I'm not the only one who hates their first name. "My brother's a Benedictine Monk at St. Gertrude's Monastery in Maryland," he replied. "Whenever I visit him, he teaches me something new. Benedictines have a strange infatuation with Saint Benedict and the history of their order."

"Well, that's narcissistic of them," Dustin muttered.

Charlie smiled at him. "It's nice to meet a lay person with this much knowledge of the history of the Church. We should sit and have a nice long discussion some time."

Roland grunted. I guess the thought of having a conversation about God with an angel was amusing to him.

My eyelids grew heavy, and I drifted off into a deep, dreamless sleep.

* * *

My brain resurfaced and I found myself staring up at the ceiling in my own bedroom.

Had it all been a dream? Could I have dreamt up the entire matter?

I sat up in my bed and felt the pain skyrocket in each and every limb. There was no way I could imagine pain of that caliber, meaning that I had to face the facts. Jenny was gone. Teddy was dead. Detective Myers was dead.

And a lot of people were hurt.

But I'm not dead.

"We were having a bet on how long it would take for you to pull through." Jenny's voice invaded my thoughts.

I looked and saw her immortalized figure staring at me with her arms crossed over her chest. "Jenny?"

She held up her hand. "I'm fine, Princess. Dustin released me from the locket right after you passed out."

I looked about, expecting to see Dustin leaning against one of the walls.

"You weren't supposed to tell her that," Teddy's ghost scowled at Jenny. He wasn't torn to shreds like he was the last time I saw him; however, he was wearing a fresh version of his ripped shirt and jeans, and his hair was ratty.

The realities hadn't quite hit me until I saw him. "You're dead."

"Yes, I am," Teddy agreed with a nod.

Tears began to flow from my eyes. "I am so sorry, Theodore, that I brought you into this mess. I never meant for—"

"It's okay, M, I'm fine with it," Teddy said, raising his hand to cut me off. "I made my peace with it, I'm just here for you to make yours."

"The demon didn't steal your soul?" I asked, trying to keep myself from sobbing.

"No, it stole my soul, it just couldn't keep hold of it when you guys obliterated it," Teddy explained with a smile.

"What do you mean?"

"Charlie is one hell of an angel," Teddy said, attempting to sit on my bed, but only managing to sink through it, which earned a laugh from Jenny.

"Charlie neglected to mention that he's not only a Guardian Angel, but also one of the first angels. When he cast out the demon, he actually destroyed it, and by doing so, released all the souls the demon captured," Jenny exclaimed enthusiastically. "You did it, Mimi! You saved us all!"

I should have been happy, I should have felt good that I'd stopped the demon, but all I could feel was numbing sadness.

"Mimi?" Jenny said, forgetting that she was a ghost. She tried to touch my hand but only managed to go right through me, sending a hundred volts of electricity through it instead. "Mimi, what's wrong?"

"You know, for the past couple months, I've been trying to convince you to cross over," I said slowly, feeling the words crushing my heart as I said each one. "And now that you're crossing over, I don't want you to leave."

A ghost of a tear slipped down Jenny's cheek. "Mimi, I won't be completely gone, not as long as you remember me. That's the good thing about friendships; it's not how much you're together, it's how much you think about each other. Besides, I'll be waiting for you when your time comes."

"We'll both be waiting," Teddy agreed, giving me a huge smile.

I looked at the them both, and I knew it was true, but I couldn't stop the sadness.

"Don't make me go all ET on you," Jenny joked, pointing her finger at the ridge of my nose.

A laugh bubbled up from my chest and I let it out, along with a couple of tears. "No need for that, I don't need any more brain trauma."

The two of them laughed, their essence flickering with each shake.

As I looked at them, I knew that this was the last conversation I was going to have with them for a very, very long time. I had no way of recording it, no way of saving it. The only way I could keep it was in my memory, and you can only trust memory so far. Of course, Jenny and Teddy didn't find it to be so bad; they had eternity. When I joined them, it would feel for them like only a moment had passed. That moment would be the rest of my life and then some, depending upon how I died and who died before me.

Teddy stepped over and placed a hand on Jenny's shoulder. "It's time to go," he said calmly. His face was gazing into the distance, as if he could see the other side of the veil between worlds.

"Don't forget about us," Jenny told me giving me one last accusing smile.

"I'll never forget, I promise," I replied, letting go of the last of my self-control.

Jenny nodded then turned to Teddy. "Are you ready?"

He nodded. "We'll see you on the other side."

I nodded, not able to respond.

"Goodbye M," Teddy said as he disappeared.

Jenny waited for a moment, then her smile faded. "Mimi, I hate to leave you without telling you the truth about what the demon really wanted from me."

"What do you mean?" I croaked, my emotions causing me to shake as I held down a sob.

"Your name. It wanted your full name, and I gave it to it."

I stared at her. "That's how it knew?"

She looked down in shame. "It threatened my family, Mimi. What would you have done in my place?"

"Are you saying that you knew it was going to kill me this entire time?" I couldn't believe what she was telling me.

"Yes. I'm ashamed of what I did, but that's why I stuck around. I couldn't let you die."

I closed my eyes and let the information sink in. I hadn't even known Dustin back before Jenny died. How could the demon have possibly known I was going to befriend him?

"I understand if you hate me, Mimi, but I couldn't cross over without letting you know. I believe someone sent that demon after you. I need you to know so that you'll be careful, alright? I can't rest peacefully until I know."

"I'll always love you, Jenny. No matter what that demon made you do. You stayed, and you saved me, risking your entire existence, and that's more than I could ask of anyone. Jenny, I don't hate you; I could never hate you. You're the best friend I've ever had."

Tears welled up in her eyes. "Bye Mimi!" Jenny waved, taking a step back and disappearing.

"Goodbye," I said as a sob rose to my throat. I didn't even bother forcing it back down, rather, I let it come out and sat there, sobbing into my blankets, completely alone for the first time in a long time.

* * *

My mom calmed down about the whole "me seeing ghosts" deal, with the help of dad's explanation and a trip to the chapel with Jenny. She still required me to go see a grief counselor, but I was okay with that, considering all the losses I experienced.

Dustin finally made peace with his friend's death, with the added visit from his friend and his parents before they crossed over. He told me they said "Thank You" for rescuing them from hell, but when I asked whether they had thanked Charlie, he blustered off onto another topic.

Charlie was able to stay and keep his position as my Guardian Angel with some help from the Big Guy. Turns out, all he had to do was ask. He's cool that way.

Detective Roland didn't arrest Dustin for all the deaths, but instead, he concocted some bogus story about how I'd been kidnapped by this serial killer and how Charlie and Dustin had been trying to save me, and were strictly, under the punishment of my death, not allowed to tell the police what was going on. Somehow, Teddy got dragged into the mess—I think they said he caught the perp with me in the back of his trunk? —and he was kidnapped and cut to shreds as well. The Detectives were confronting Dustin at his house when out of nowhere, the unsub attacked, killing Myers and knocking Dustin out. Charlie followed the guy to the cemetery, where he found me and a dead Teddy, then phoned Roland. Charlie was fending off the unsub when Roland shot at him three times, hitting him once, but he got away. We figure he's trying to get over the border now, so there's no need to worry about him attacking anyone in Adam's Grove ever again.

"What a great story," I told Dustin once he finished relaying it to me for the first time. We were sitting in the park on the bench where we had our first actual conversation. It was finally hot, and most of the little kids were enjoying their time running in and out of the cold river water only a couple hundred meters away.

"I thought you would appreciate the art involved in it," he replied with a laugh. "Oh, and you were knocked out the entire time, just in case anybody asks you what the guy looked like."

"Detective Roland made sure to make you sound very lame," I pointed out.

"Yeah, well, he can have his 'official' story, and I'll have the one I tell around town saying how he ran when he saw the guy, and I stayed back and fought until I was heroically knocked out by a bookshelf."

"You jumped on the demon's back and expected to accomplish something," I reminded him, bringing his ego back into check. "I was the one who imprisoned it the first time."

"Details, details," he said with a wave of his hand.

"Charlie sounds very heroic," I noticed almost with surprise.

Dustin's face darkened. "Of course, he does, Demetrius and he are getting along like best buds."

"Would you please use his last name?" I asked.

"Absolutely not! Have you ever said 'Demetrius' before? It comes off your tongue like a super bowl party. Say it! Demetrius, Demetrius," he continued to say the name as if he were singing. "Give it a whirl!"

"This is what you did when you first discovered my first name, isn't it?"

"Possibly, but you'd have to ask Charlie about it."

"Poor Charlie and Detective Roland."

"It's not 'poor Charlie and Detective Roland'," Dustin said, completely astounded. "You should see them together, it's sickening."

"Aww, does somebody feel unloved?" I said with fake sympathy, grabbing his hand in mine.

"I did all the work saving you! Sure, he saved you when we were in the chapel, and sure he cast out the demon and cured you of poison, but I saved you in the alley, I saved you from the river, I saved you from freezing to death. Hell, I even saved you from being captured, and the only credit I get is being the main suspect and getting knocked out. Stupid cops." Dustin pouted, but didn't let go of my hand.

"If it makes you feel better, I know what you did, and I think you were very heroic," I said, leaning my head against his shoulder. "I'd be dead if it weren't for you."

His smile faded. "If I hadn't shown up—" he began.

"Oh, not this again!" I cut him off, moving back into a sitting position. "Dustin Harold Harper, you could not have prevented the events that unfolded by not have coming to Michigan. It only would have changed the people and the location. We've been through this before."

"But if I hadn't grabbed the necklace off the bottom of the river—"

"You thought it was your mother's!"

"But it wasn't now, was it? It belonged to a demon, the very one who killed both of my parents and my best friend, and your best friend, and your ex-boyfriend, Detective Myers, and the nice hobo who lived down the street from school. It all comes down to one decision that I made."

I took a deep breath and sighed. "But if you hadn't grabbed the locket, who knows how countless many more lives the demon would have taken. It was so focused on getting the locket back that it was willing to give up its ploy—its entire existence—just to get it back. We took it down, razed it, Dustin. That demon is gone now because of your actions. Millennia of captured souls have now been released, able to cross over because of your marvelous deed! Can you not find some peace in that?"

"Um, about that," Dustin released my hand and turned his head so that I couldn't look him in the eyes.

"What about it?" I asked him, my suspicions aroused.

"Well, we did release a couple millennia worth of captured souls," Dustin said, carefully choosing each word.

"And?" I pressed.

"Well, not all of those souls are—how should I put this? —necessarily peaceful."

"What?" I said, my dread coming back.

He shifted uncomfortably, wringing his hands as he spoke, and tensing up as if someone were about to hit him. "Meems, you had to see it coming. I mean, think of how many souls this demon took! It didn't care who this person was when it took their soul, all it wanted was another soul to add to its collection, whether it be bad or good. In this case, we released all the souls, good *and* bad."

"Well, aren't the bad souls taken directly to hell?" I asked.

"Usually, if they die under normal circumstances."

"Dustin—!"

"I've already started compiling a list of troubles that have arisen since we defeated the demon. I figure they're linked, in one way or another, to our newfound escaped inmates." He pulled out a list, one that rolled out and across the humid grass for a couple of feet. "This should keep us busy for a while, I've been getting word from all around the country."

"You've got to be kidding me," I said as I took the list out of his hands and stared at it myself.

"No, I'm not kidding you. These are just the ones in this small stretch of Michigan," Dustin replied, leaning back onto the bench. "So, which one would you like to take a look at first? I'm not sure which ones of these things are the real deal, but I'm sure if we scope them out for ourselves, we'll be able to determine it."

"Do we really have to capture every single soul that's on this list?" I asked, not believing my eyes. There were so many places, so many possibilities. How could we possibly capture them all?

"Well, we did set them loose on the populous," Dustin reminded me, once again tensing up as if I were about to punch him, "and we are quite well equipped for handling this sort of phenomenon. I think it's our civic duties as Mortuus Loquis to put our feelers out and track down each and every evil spirit that got loose due to our fight with the devil. It's only what's right."

I stared at the list that ran on and on; there was no way in hell we could ever accomplish this list, not when we still had to deal with all the other departed souls who were trapped on this plane. More and more of them come each day.

"It's not like we have to do this all in one day," Dustin continued. "It'll take years just to blot out all the false reports. And then we have to deal with school and everything, but we can take weekend trips and we can go to the places that need our help most first. Come on, Matilda, what do you say?" He stared at me with his puppy-dog golden eyes.

"I say," I began as my eyes picked up something on the list, "that I will not go to any haunted houses, canneries, or butcher shops with just you as backup."

Dustin's eyes lit up. "Oh, it won't be just us," he said, jumping to his feet. "Charlie said he'll come with us on all our trips, and your dad said he'll join us if need be. Your mom got our legal defense ready if we ever need it, my uncle has our expenses, and Detective Roland has got friends all over the state. He got a promotion in the FBI as well—did you know he's FBI? He was trained at Quantico before he moved here and was assigned a mission in deep cover to investigate the spike in suicides in Chicago, then here in Adam's Creek. He worked at a field office in Chicago, which is how he got so much information on my past. Can you believe it? But anyways, he took a position on the 'Abnormal' task force division, which looks into all the oddities in life. He said we can call him if ever we need some help."

"It seems that you weren't going to take no for an answer," I said, rolling up the list as to rise to my feet.

"Well, I was going to take it, but then I'd ask until you'd say yes," Dustin admitted with a triumphant smile. "We're going to fulfil our purpose in this life."

I handed him the roll and tried to sound annoyed. "You think our purpose is to go around, city to city, and hunt down every last aberration that we come across?"

"Absolutely," he answered with a nod. "We've already passed our first test."

"Our first test?"

"Yeah, the demon. You say God has everything happen for a reason. Well, this is that reason, Meems; I vote we go with it."

I bit my lip and rolled my eyes; I hate it when he has a good point. "Where to first?" I asked.

Dustin let the list fall freely to the ground. "Whatever place catches your eye," he replied.

I glared at him, annoyed that he had already undone my work of rolling the list. "So, you want me to pick first?"

He nodded.

"Alright," I said, giving the list a quick glance. "How about somewhere close by, like the ghost of White Pine Mine. That sounds like a fun one."

Dustin shook his head and said, "That's apparently going to be rather difficult. I hear it's quite a . . . gruesome case. We should probably test out something a little bit simpler the first time."

"Fine, why not the warring tree on Apricot Hill?"

He rolled up the list. "Alright, let's go."

"You're serious?" I said, rather surprised. "You want to go right now?"

"Mmm hmm. Best get ahead of it while we still have a chance." He began walking towards his car parked on the curb.

I looked around at the little playground that stood before me. It seemed so long ago that he warned me that I could chose each situation that I walked into, that nobody was forcing me to make the choices that I make. I could always choose to tuck-and-roll out of the passenger's side. Now I was sitting in that car again with the decision to sit along for the ride and see where it takes me, or to tuck-and-roll.

"Dustin, wait up!" I called as I ran after him into the humid air of early July.

Made in the USA
Monee, IL
20 November 2023

46871081R00100